The Contemporary C...

GYÖRGY LIGETI

The Contemporary Composers

Series Editor: Nicholas Snowman

GYÖRGY LIGETI

Paul Griffiths

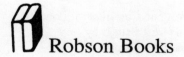
Robson Books

Acknowledgements
The musical examples, which are printed at sounding pitch, are reproduced by kind permission of Universal Edition (Example 1), Peters Edition Ltd. (Examples 2 and 3), and Schott Musik International GmbH (Examples 4–12).

FIRST PUBLISHED IN GREAT BRITAIN IN 1983 BY ROBSON BOOKS LTD., THIS EDITION PUBLISHED IN 1997   BY ROBSON BOOKS LTD. BOLSOVER HOUSE, 5-6 CLIPSTONE STREET, LONDON W1P 8LE.

British Library Cataloguing in Publication Data
Griffiths, Paul

ISBN 1 86105 058 5

Typeset by The Harrington Consultancy, London
Printed and bound in Great Britain by
Hartnolls Ltd., Bodmin, Cornwall

Contents

Editor's Preface to the First Edition

It is no secret that our epoch favours a museological rather than a prospective approach to musical activity. Such a situation is, of course, the reflection of a cultural climate, but it is also the result of problems particular to the evolution of musical language during this century.

Whatever the fundamental causes, the effects are clear. The repertoire of classical music has been extended backwards in time and enlarged with the inclusion of many important works as well as a great number of lesser ones. At the same time the standard works of the eighteenth and nineteenth centuries have become more than ever entrenched in a musical world very largely conditioned by market considerations and thus inimical to contemporary endeavour. One cannot blame record company employees, concert promoters and artists' agents for being more interested in quick turnover than in the culture of their time. The results are inevitable: re-recordings of the same symphonies and operas multiply; performances of the same early music, claiming to be less inauthentic than their rivals, abound; and conductors' careers are made with an ever-diminishing bunch of scores.

Where does this leave the music written yesterday and today? The answer is not encouraging. As far as western Europe and the United States are concerned, contemporary works inhabit a number of well-defined ghettos.

In West Germany it is the radio stations that commission and perform new scores and, naturally enough, their concern is to satisfy their specialist listeners rather than to cultivate a wider public. Except for a certain number of important but brief shop window festivals, contemporary music is hardly a living affair.

In the United States composers find sanctuary in the universities – comfort and security but little contact with the general musical public outside the walls, whilst symphony orchestras, reliant for their existence on the whims of the rich and generally conservative, tend to play safe.

In the UK, outside the BBC and one or two imaginative enterprises the situation is depressing – on the one hand, inadequate state funds spread too thinly, on the other, excellent but hungry orchestras competing for the same marketable fodder. Indeed, at the moment there is not even a modest but representative contemporary music festival worthy of international attention.

France, with its rigorous but narrow education system giving little place to the non-literary arts, has suddenly in the last few years woken up to the charms of music and begun to invest more and more heavily in this new passion. Yet in spite of all the talk and activity, contemporary music outside Paris attracts small audiences; the work of decentralisation so dear to Gallic politicians is more arduous here than in other countries.

This is not the place for a thorough survey of the status of contemporary music in the world in general. However, it seems clear that even a brief glance at a few different countries reveals the existence of an uneasy relationship between the contemporary public and its music. Certainly, a few independently minded and cultivated musicians seek by their artistic policies to persuade the musical public to accept the endeavours of the present as well as the rich and varied musical traditions and structures of the past.

This new series of books, each introducing a different living composer, seeks to supplement the work of the pathfinders. The scope of the series does not reflect any particular musical party line or aesthetic; its aims are to be representative of what exists, and to supply the listener who stumbles across a new piece at a Prom or on record with the essential facts about its composer – his life, background and work.

Nicholas Snowman
Paris, June 1981

Editor's Preface to the Second Edition

The Contemporary Composers series was first launched some fifteen years ago. In that time exceptional changes have taken place in the world of classical music. The traditional concert with its established repertoire based mainly in the 18th and 19th centuries is now showing signs of vulnerability, whereas contemporary music is flourishing in a way that would have been difficult to imagine in the early 1980s.

Until relatively recently music-lovers had to come to concerts to hear unfamiliar repertoire. With the arrival of CDs, and in particular budget price reissues of superlative and celebrated recordings, acquainting oneself with, for example, a lesser known Dvořák symphony has become a far easier task than it was when there was no alternative but to catch a live performance. Now the public quite rightly wishes to experience major events rather than run of the mill evenings of classical or, indeed, any other music. The future must surely lie in the presentation of fewer but more stimulating concerts.

These past fifteen years have also seen the arrival in prominent positions of conductors with a greater sense of adventure and idealism than most of their predecessors. The two most potent symbols of status quo and tradition in classical music, the Berlin Philharmonic and the Vienna Philharmonic, have both undergone profound transformation. Not only are these orchestras now conducted by a range of musicians representing a new breadth of interpretative styles, but the players themselves have responded remarkably to change as well as bringing fresh young talent into their own ranks.

These changes are particularly marked in the United Kingdom

where symphony orchestras have moved from simply replaying the established canon of works to a broader repertoire including pieces from the post-Second World War and contemporary eras. Before, such repertoire had been left largely to the BBC. Now distinguished festivals devoted to contemporary work exist in Huddersfield and the Vale of Glamorgan, whilst arts centres and concert halls up and down the country demonstrate that the contemporary is ever more integrated with the traditional.

These developments are matched in the record industry. Though the attractiveness of reasonably priced reissues has rendered the endless rerecording of standard works uneconomical, this situation has encouraged companies to investigate the distant past as well as the present far more imaginatively than before. Of course, financial constraints are increasingly to be felt world-wide, but it is most encouraging to sense the new vigour in the promotion of contemporary work internationally.

When these books were first launched, not only was the situation for contemporary music less healthy than today but some of the composers we featured, for example, Birtwistle, Ligeti and Maxwell Davies, whilst known to a specialist international audience, were not the familiar names they have now become. Hopefully, this series will continue to play a modest but precise role in increasing the enjoyment of the music it celebrates.

                                              Nicholas Snowman
                                        London, November 1996

Introduction to the First Edition

In an earlier book in this series, on Peter Maxwell Davies, I began with an anecdote concerning my own introduction to his music, at a string quartet recital in an Oxford college. The first time I heard any Ligeti came only a little later, but under rather different circumstances, in a London cinema at a showing of Stanley Kubrick's film *2001: A Space Odyssey*. The effect, though, was similar, and my initial disappointment that Ligeti had not written dozens of Requiems and *Atmosphères* quickly turned into joy that he had written works of different kinds no less extraordinary. I hope this book will do a little to spread that pleasure: again the dedication is some repayment for a debt of education, for it is through performances by the London Sinfonietta that I have learned a great deal about Ligeti (not to mention Stockhausen, Berio, Boulez, Henze, Birtwistle, Davies, Schoenberg, Stravinsky . . .).

I am also very grateful for the loan of scores to Sally Groves of Schott, Graham Hayter of Peters Edition and Frances White of Universal Edition.

Paul Griffiths
1983

Introduction to the
Second Edition

During the thirteen years since the first edition of this book, Ligeti's output has grown in two directions, forwards and backwards. There has been a wonderful flowering of new works, including the Piano Concerto, the Violin Concerto, the Viola Sonata and the continuing series of Piano Etudes. And there has been, almost as wonderfully, a retrieval of music from the past – an archaeological exploration that has exposed much more of Ligeti's music from before he left Hungary in 1956. The new early Ligeti must now be included in the story, of course – but which story? My solution – which is to consider the music, new and old, roughly in order of western publication – will, I hope, justify itself in the telling. Composers, like all of us, live their lives in chronological order, but their music can support – even insist on – alternatives. Of course, those alternatives are manifold, and an adequate Ligeti book would have to be as polyphonic as his music habitually is – would have, for example, to treat the works of the late fifties and early sixties as a bolt from the blue, occasioned by an abrupt change of musical climate, and as a direct outcome of what he had been writing in Hungary. The interview I recorded with the composer for the first edition may, perhaps, make up a little for the homophony of my prose – especially at points of conflict with the composer's later view, as represented by the catalogue at the end of the book.

I am happy to acknowledge again the assistance I have had from Ligeti's publishers, especially Sally Groves (Schott London) and Bernhard Pfau (Schott Mainz). Alongside them I greet Louise Duchesneau, the composer's assistant, who has been generously helpful, encouraging and warm, and to whom I am very much indebted, as I am, indeed, to Ligeti himself, who has taken the trouble to correct my list of his works, which thereby includes many details not previously available, and which also, for the first time, indicates which compositions he considers definitive.

Paul Griffiths
1996

Part one

East

Interview with the Composer

Like the fabled Count Dracula and the real Prince Vlad, György Sándor Ligeti is a Transylvanian, born on 28 May 1923 in a territory that had been part of Hungary until the division of the Habsburg empire at the end of the First World War, and that was now within the boundaries of Romania. Here as elsewhere in central Europe the frequent changes of frontier and the mixture of peoples have brought a certain instability to place names: Ligeti's home town was known as Dicsőszentmárton to its Hungarian population (among them his parents) and as Diciosânmărtin to its Romanians; now it is Tîrnăveni. But Ligeti did not spend long there. Soon after his birth the family moved to the provincial centre of Kolozsvár (or Cluj to Romanians), and there he had his schooling and early musical education. He studied at the conservatory from 1941 to 1943 under Ferenc Farkas, a pupil of Respighi and one of the most distinguished Hungarian composers of the post-Bartók generation. At the same time, during the summers, he had private lessons in Budapest with another outstanding figure in Hungarian music at the time, Pál Kadosa, who belonged to the school of Kodály.

The later war years put an end for the moment to this orthodox development of a young composer. As a Jew in Nazi Hungary Ligeti was in trouble: he survived by great good luck in a labour camp; his father and his brother he never saw again. Then after the war he returned to his studies, now at the alma mater of Bartók and Kodály, the Academy of Music in Budapest, where his teachers included Farkas again and two other leading composers of the same generation, Sándor Veress and Pál Járdányi, both of them also pupils of Kodály. All the time he was composing. He had had his first publication back in 1942, when a song of his, 'Kineret' (the Hebrew name for the Sea of Galilee), had won a competition. His second work to appear in print was a little chorus, published not only in Cluj and Budapest but also, curiously, in London, where the Workers' Music Association brought it out under the title 'Early Comes the Summer' in 1947. It would be too much, though, to suggest that at this stage he was gaining an international reputation. His more substantial and more ambitious compositions all remained unpublished, and indeed that remained the case for as long as he was in Hungary.

In 1949 he graduated from the academy and in Hungary the screw of Stalinist dictatorship turned tighter. For a young composer the only accepted creative outlet was in the direction of choral songs and folksong arrangements, and these Ligeti produced, but he also, while now teaching at the academy, went on in search of more challenging material to set down in works he knew could never be performed. He knew too that his more adventurous ideas were taking him into areas where he could have been helped by music that had been placed under interdict: little of Schoenberg was available to him, nothing of Webern, and even the knottier scores of Bartók himself were proscribed. In 1953 there came a slight thaw, and then in 1956, with the revolution, a much greater access of freedom, until the arrival of the Russian tanks that November. Ligeti, like many of his countrymen, then left Hungary for the west, and the eastern composer – the still mysterious figure who taught at the academy, made folksong arrangements and struggled clandestinely to live musically in the present day instead of in the folksy never-never land of official music – that composer suddenly at the age of thirty-three became the 'real' Ligeti.

This is the outline. It remains to be filled in with the composer's own reminiscences, recorded in an interview on 1 December 1982, the evening before the British première of his opera *Le Grand Macabre*.

PG: *Could you say when you first had the idea that you were going to be a composer?*

GL: In my childhood I didn't have any such idea. I wanted to play an instrument – I particularly wanted to play the violin – but my father was against it, and it wasn't until I was fourteen that I started to play the piano. It was pretty late, which means that I don't have a very good technique. And that's a pity, because I love to play the piano.

Actually, it was because of my brother that I got the chance to start. Somebody told him that he had absolute pitch and ought to play an instrument, and so he started the violin when he was nine. Then I could insist that I should have music lessons as well, and so I started on the piano because he was playing the violin. Though we didn't have a piano in the house. I had to go every day to a friend of my mother's to practise.

Then I composed immediately after starting to learn the piano. I remember exactly: I was fourteen, maybe fourteen and a half, and my first piece was a waltz in the style of Grieg, because one of the very easy Lyrical Pieces is a waltz. But the decision that I was a composer, that only came much later, and very gradually. Of course I was writing a lot of compositions, but totally naïve.

When I was eighteen the intention was that I should go to the university to study physics, but by that time – it was 1941 – the anti-Jewish laws had been passed, and it was very, very difficult for a Jew to enter the university. So my father said: 'All right, you can go to the conservatory.' And one year after that I decided: no more science. I would be a composer.

That meant studying everything from the beginning, right back to tonic-dominant harmony, because I had absolutely no music theory at that stage. I could play the piano a little bit – not very well, because I had only been playing for three years or so. But I was accepted into the composition class at the conservatory because I had so many compositions.

*You mentioned there something about your family background; I
wonder if you could say a little more.*

We were an absolutely middle-class family. My mother was an
ophthalmologist; she died only this year. It's difficult to say what
my father was, because his life changed several times, and not
because he wanted it to. He studied economics at Budapest
University and then joined a bank, as a manager of a small
branch. This was in Romania. Then there came the crisis of
1929–30, and the small private banks were all abolished. My
father carried on working in the same office, but the office
changed, and instead of being a banker he became the manager of
a small office selling state lottery tickets. He hated it.

But in fact he was also a writer: he wrote several books on
economics, from a radical socialist point of view. He was very
much to the left. And of course when the anti-Jewish laws came
in he lost his job and was eventually taken off to Auschwitz,
along with my mother and my brother. My mother was the only
one of them to come back.

Your father wasn't musical?

Oh yes, he was quite, quite musical. He'd studied the violin in his
youth. He only didn't want me to study music because it had been
no use to him.

It was an artistic family. My grandfather, my father's father,
was a painter – not a famous painter, but a sort of high-level
decorator, painting murals in railway stations and so on. And
there was one famous musician, the violinist Leopold Auer, who
was my father's uncle. I never met him: he was in America when
I was born, and he died in 1930. My grandfather too was an Auer.
All Germans and Jews in Hungary tended to have German
names, but then in the 1890s it became the fashion to take
Hungarian names – it was part of the nationalist movement at that

time. My father and his brothers were then at school, and they decided to change the name to 'Ligeti'. It's a false translation: an 'Aue' in German is a water meadow, and 'liget' in Hungarian means a small wood.

How did you manage to escape your father's and your brother's fate during the war?

I had to go for military service in January 1944. For Jews this meant forced labour: we were put into labour camps that were part of the Hungarian army. We were considered enemies and had no uniforms; instead we were marked as Jews with yellow armbands, and of course we had no weapons. The other unreliable minorities, like the Romanians, the Ukrainians and the Serbs, were also put into labour corps, but the Jews had a worse status: effectively that of prisoners of war. We were also forced to do excessive and dangerous work: for instance, my unit had to transport heavy explosives to the front line. When I began my military service the deportation of the Jews from Hungary had not yet begun – that happened in June 1944 – and my parents were still at home, living under all the anti-Jewish restrictions.

They were in Romania?

No, they were in Hungary. To tell you exactly, I was born in this small town of Dicsőszentmárton, which was right in the middle of Transylvania, and which was and still is in Romania. Then when I was six we moved to Cluj, the main city of Transylvania, where I started going to the opera and so on. That was also in Romania, but in 1940, when I was seventeen, Hitler divided Transylvania in two parts and gave the northern half, including Cluj, to Hungary. So then we were Hungarians. After the war, of course, Cluj went back to Romania, but by that time I was already in Budapest.

The government at the time I was called up for the labour corps was secretly making plans with the British, but the Germans got to know about it and installed a puppet government on 19 March 1944: that was when the physical elimination of the Jews started. The German forces came in, like the Russians in Hungary later or Czechoslovakia, occupying an allied country. But in the new pro-Hitler government there was just at that time a man in the defence ministry who wanted to protect the Jews who were in the service of the army, and so some people who had been called up in the winter of 1943–4 were saved: those who came earlier or later died. So it was quite a chance that I escaped, though I didn't realize it till afterwards.

In October 1944 I deserted from the labour corps in the front line during a battle. Again I was lucky not to be taken prisoner by the Russians. I went back on foot to Transylvania, which was then under Russian occupation, and the last half-year of the war I spent there.

And then immediately after the war you went to Budapest to study.

Yes, the war was finished in May 1945, and I went to Budapest in September.

What sort of music were you writing by then?

I was very much impressed by Bartók. You know, he was the great Hungarian composer, and I knew very little other modern music: a little bit of Stravinsky – *Petrushka* but not yet *Le sacre* – no Schoenberg. Bartók was the big genius: I think he still is, for me.

I have several of those early pieces. The style isn't totally Bartók: you know, when you are young you oscillate a bit, so there are also some little Stravinsky influences. Even my first string quartet, from 1953–4, is still Bartók.

It's also Ligeti.

Yes, a little bit, but it was not conscious. And the Six Bagatelles for wind are also Bartók with a little Stravinsky. Later in the fifties I began very gradually to come towards a Ligeti style. But of course the political situation was very complex, and the political situation went into the composing. I was then very much committed to the left, though I was never a communist (I'm not left-wing any more because experience has . . .). Anyway, I was a radical socialist, and there were many of us who wanted to believe that Soviet communism was one way to create a socialist system. I had a lot of sympathy with that, being so very left and having so many friends who were, and they convinced me that I ought to write music that, you know, everybody can understand.

So I forced it a little bit. At the beginning I really wanted to come away from this chromatic style and come more towards a sort of Hungarian folk style – not really Kodály, but somewhere between Bartók and Kodály. There were so many composers doing that, and when you are young you want to belong to a group. In fact, even in 1945 I had written a little choral piece in Kodály style: it was the only piece of mine that was translated into English and printed here . . .

'Early Comes the Summer'.

Yes, a very naïve piece. So in this kind of style I wrote a lot of choral pieces, but I was divided: at the same time I was writing chamber pieces and songs that were more complex, more radical.

Those more radical pieces would include the Weöres songs of 1946–7?

Yes, they are maybe as radical as Bartók is. There were three of them, but I have only two.[1] One day I will publish them.

Afterwards, in 1947–8, I wanted to write a very simple, diatonic music, because I believed that music ought to be more popular. Then in 1949 the Soviets imprisoned the majority of the deputies and imposed a puppet communist government. From 1948 to 1949 everyday life changed radically: the totalitarian Stalinist dictatorship began. It was terrible; it was really like the Nazis. This was the time of Zhdanov in Russia.

So any new kind of music was prohibited, which made things difficult in Hungary because Bartók was the great national composer. They didn't want to prohibit Bartók, and so his name was kept, but at concerts or on the radio you heard only the first string quartet or the sixth string quartet. They were tolerated, but the second quartet to the fifth not, the Music for Strings not. The *Mandarin* was in the repertory at the opera, and from one day to the next they put it away. The list of people who were prohibited even included Britten or Darius Milhaud.

It was a very bad situation, and I became an anti-communist. It wasn't just a matter of cultural policy: people were just disappearing into concentration camps, or prison, or being killed. It was a terrible time from 1948 until the death of Stalin in 1953. And I had a very strong feeling that I had to write radically new music, not this kind of pseudo-popular music, though all the time I was writing Hungarian folksong arrangements and choruses that were even performed and even published. But only those pieces: not the more complex compositions like the quartet and the bagatelles.

It was in 1949 that you wrote a big youth cantata. Was that before or after the new regime came into power?

I began it before, in the summer of 1948. It was in a very popular style, a sort of Kodály-Handel-Britten style. There was a big fugue: I was very good at counterpoint. And it was absolutely what I wanted: completely diatonic, though not tonal but modal. The text was against imperialism and all those things, and I believed in it, at that moment. It was my graduation piece from the academy.

It was performed in 1949 at a World Youth Festival, which was a communist event, only we didn't know that: I was completely naïve – I didn't realize what happens. My cantata was perhaps closest to Britten's *Spring Symphony*: Britten was extremely popular in Hungary immediately after the war and until 1949. And when I began the work it was something totally honest. When it was performed, a year later, in 1949, I was completely against the regime.

You have to understand how much it was a time of transformation. So many people believed in this utopia, and then they were so completely disappointed – more than disappointed.

But I have the score, and maybe one day it will be performed again.

Then for a while your works were mostly on a small scale, though I'm intrigued by one title from 1951, your 'Grand symphonie militaire' op.69.

Oh that was a joke: the opus number refers of course to the sexual position. No, this was a very bad time, when I had no pieces performed, and a friend of mine called Melles – he conducted the youth cantata – had an orchestra of the postmen in Budapest. They wanted a piece, and as a joke I made a little sonata form in Haydn-Stravinsky style, or like the Prokofiev 'Classical' Symphony, but very ironical, and a little bit ironical against the political situation. They gave it a rehearsal so that I could hear it, but it was never performed in a concert.

At the same time, though, you were writing more 'serious' works.

Yes. There was a set of Arany [a famous Hungarian poet] songs
which I wrote in 1952 and which were on the edge of what could
be performed. Finally they were not performed.

You know, it's very difficult to understand if you are not in it.
Every composer had to be a member of the composers' union:
you had to be in order to get hold of manuscript paper. If you
wanted a performance or publication, you had to submit your
work to a committee, and there might even be a private
performance for that committee: that happened with my Arany
songs. Then you would be informed if they wanted to broadcast
the music, or whatever. You couldn't ask. My Arany songs were
something between Bartók and Kodály, with some dissonances,
and they were not acceptable.

But the most interesting thing from this point of view was my
Six Bagatelles for wind quintet. The sixth is a chromatic piece,
and there was no possibility of these pieces being performed
when I wrote them in 1953. But in 1956 there was a festival and
they performed the first five: the sixth was still too chromatic and
dissonant even for those times.

By that time the political situation was very much more relaxed.

Oh yes. Until 1953, I can say, we were completely isolated from
the west, or maybe until 1954. I had an uncle in London, and we
corresponded with each other, but after 1949 it was dangerous to
write letters to western countries: anybody who was not
regarded as reliable by the government was taken away from
Budapest – maybe 200,000 people – and their flats were
confiscated. But in 1955 it began to become possible for me to
receive scores and records from abroad, and so I began to know
Schoenberg. I had seen scores of the Schoenberg second quartet
and the Berg Lyric Suite in the library of the music academy, but

if you have never heard that kind of music . . .

It was also in 1955 that I heard Bartók's third and fourth quartets for the first time. In those last two years in Budapest, 1955 and 1956, very gradually I came to know all of Bartók, more of Stravinsky, and some Schoenberg: I heard the third and fourth string quartets on record, and *Pierrot lunaire*. I hadn't had a record player for LPs – they weren't being produced in Hungary at the time – and I couldn't hear these records until cheap West German record players began to be imported in 1955 or maybe 1956.

But you could hear radio broadcasts.

Yes, except that they were being jammed. For instance, the first time I heard a Stockhausen piece was during the revolution, because jamming was stopped. It was on 7 November 1956 and it was the first broadcast of *Gesang der Jünglinge*. The Soviets had come in and everybody was down in the cellars, but I went up so that I could hear the music clearly. There were detonations going on, and shrapnel, so it was quite dangerous to be listening.

You haven't yet published much of the music you yourself were writing at this time.

The Six Bagatelles are published, and two choral pieces, and the first quartet will be: I only have to correct the proofs. But everything will be published. It's only my laziness that has held these pieces back. And I have most of what I wrote, except for pieces written before the war: even the works that are described as lost in Nordwall's catalogue, they turn up.

Were you starting to write serial music before you left Hungary?

Not serial in the sense of Boulez and Stockhausen, but using rows, yes. It was a very short time, the time when I heard the third and fourth quartets of Schoenberg, and also Webern's op.5 pieces for string quartet. I had this period in 1955–6 when I wrote twelve-tone music, because, you know, this was the most 'modern' style, and it was part of liberating myself from Bartók. And maybe I got there by listening to Schoenberg, but stylistically they are not Schoenberg, and not Webern either. There was a Chromatic Fantasy for piano – I think it's a very bad piece – which is absolutely orthodox twelve-tone music.

I also began a twelve-tone Requiem in 1956: this was the second time I'd started a Requiem, before the Requiem I wrote in the sixties. Of course, this was a time when everyone, in the west and in the east, wanted to write twelve-tone music, and I was too young to realize that twelve-tone music was nothing for me. Then later in 1956, still in Budapest, I knew what I wanted to do, but immediately before I hadn't – except in those two choral pieces, *Evening* and *Morning*, from 1955, which are not twelve-tone but also not any more Bartók.

There was another piece which maybe today I might try to continue, and that was an oratorio to words by the same poet, Sándor Weöres, on the ancient Babylonian legend of Istar. I composed the prelude, which was a passacaglia on a twelve-tone theme, and a little bit what I am doing now rhythmically, having different layers in different metres, like in the pieces for two pianos. This was the first example of it, completely twelve-tone and rhythmically machine-like.

But you know I was so naïve then. I first read about twelve-tone music in 1956 in a book of Jelinek – absolutely not interesting, but then it was something new. The years 1955–6 were so important as a transition, the two years before I left Hungary and went to Cologne, and really began to write my own music, though I had started already in Budapest, in that orchestral piece *Víziók*.

That's not twelve-tone?

No, no. It's just chromatic clusters, exactly the same as the first movement of *Apparitions*.

How did you leave Hungary?

During the revolution it was very easy to leave, because the frontiers were open, but we believed that now everything would be all right: just like the Czechs and then the Poles. I left fairly late, in December 1956, by which time the Soviet control had been consolidated, and the Hungarian police and military had been completely obliterated. Everything was controlled by the Soviets, and they had enough people to put a ring around Budapest.

But the railway people organized trains for people who wanted to go in the direction of the Austrian frontier: of course they never arrived at the frontier. The train stopped at every station, and they telephoned ahead to the next station to find out if there were Russian soldiers there: this was perfectly possible, because the telephone wasn't controlled. It was chaos, but all the time the telephone functioned. Even during the battles you could telephone London if you wanted.

I and my wife took the train one day, and we got to a town in west Hungary about sixty kilometres from the border. There had been some mistake and the warning had failed: the train was surrounded by the Russian military. But they didn't have enough people to cover the whole train. Within seconds they took away everybody from the front half of the train, but we in our end very quickly got out and into the town. Somebody told us to go to the post office, where we could be hidden overnight: it was very well organized. And the next day the postman took us on by train, just an engine and a mail wagon, with ten or twelve people hidden under the mailbags. It was quite dangerous, because there was a three-year-old child with us, and he had to be given tablets to make him sleep.

Then we were dropped quite close to the frontier, not in a station but outside, and we were told to get out and do what we could. It was perhaps ten kilometres from the border, and already within the prohibited zone, with Russians patrolling. Then the next night somebody showed us the frontier, while all the time the Russians were lighting up the sky with rockets. We knew we had reached the border when we fell into the mud where the mines had been: the mines had been cleared during the revolution, because Austria refused to have trade with Hungary while the border was mined.

So it was a big chance.

You then went quite soon to Cologne.

Yes. While I was in Budapest I had been in correspondence with Herbert Eimert and with Stockhausen, the directors of the electronic music studio, and they helped to organize a scholarship for me. I went there about six weeks later, at the beginning of February 1957.

And then you started work on your electronic pieces.

Not at once. First of all I did an analysis of Boulez's *Structures*, which was later published in *Die Reihe*.

Had you wanted to compose electronic music when you were in Hungary?

No, there was no possibility: you know, at that time there were only five or six electronic studios in the world. I had this fascination, to know what electronic music is, and I had heard *Gesang der Jünglinge.*

Then in Cologne I composed three pieces, *Glissandi, Artikulation* and a third piece called *Atmosphères* which was never realized.

Was that related to the orchestral Atmosphères?

No, absolutely not. There was something that became the idea of micropolyphony in the orchestral piece, but the electronic piece was not a cluster composition but to do with harmonics and combination tones. I never finished it because it turned out to be too complicated: there were forty-eight layers, and we couldn't put them together without getting too much noise. Today it would be very simple with digital techniques.

You've never gone back to electronic music.

No. I wanted to, but life . . .

Do you still want to?

Maybe today not, but this is really a personal matter. Five years ago I became ill. If I were to go into electronics I would need three years to learn programming, and how to deal with computers in general, because I would want to do everything myself, so I decided to renounce that field. But still, even without working with computers, in my musical thinking generally, I'm very influenced by this idea of feedback between technology and the imagination, by the kind of thinking that's natural if you work with computers.

Was there anything more specific that you gained from your work in the electronic studio in 1957–8?

Oh yes, the idea of micropolyphonic webs was a sort of inspiration that I got from working in the studio, putting pieces together layer by layer. I was very much influenced too by older music, by the very complex polyphony of Ockeghem, for example: after all, I had been a teacher of counterpoint. But it was the studio work that gave me the technique. For instance, I had to read up psychoacoustics at that time, and I learned that if you have a sequence of sounds where the difference in time is less than fifty milliseconds then you don't hear them any more as individual sounds. This gave me the idea of creating a very close succession in instrumental music, and I did that in the second movement of *Apparitions* and in *Atmosphères*. But the idea of a completely static music, like in the first movement of *Apparitions*, that was something I'd had in Budapest. This kind of cluster thinking I think came probably from the area of Bartók, much more than from the Viennese. For me, though, yes, it was something quite new.

Part Two

West

Although the timing of Ligeti's emigration was dictated by political events in Hungary, this was a useful hour for any gifted composer to be arriving in Germany – Mauricio Kagel came from Argentina at roughly the same time, and also to Cologne – for 1956 was high-noontime for the musical avant garde. Leading young composers all over western Europe felt themselves at this point to belong to a unified phalanx, defined partly by allegiance to certain principles (the structuring of music according to objective criteria, the need for constant innovation), and partly by opposition to any compromise with the past. They were men (exclusively men) of Ligeti's own generation: Bruno Maderna was three years older and Luigi Nono just a few months younger, while Pierre Boulez and Luciano Berio were two years his junior and Karlheinz Stockhausen five. And these people – all of them around thirty – were the senior figures. They met each summer at the holiday courses in new music held in Darmstadt (where Ligeti was regularly present from 1957 to 1966, and intermittently during the next decade); they also encountered one another at the festivals where their works were performed, most of these festivals being supported by the well-funded German broadcasting authorities, and so taking place in German cities (Donaueschingen, Cologne, Bremen, Hamburg, Munich). The young composers of this German-centred but international group had by 1956 gained the support of discipleship from a still younger generation, and even from their most distinguished ancestor, Stravinsky, who was moving rapidly towards them along his own track. Their latest works immediately had the status of modern classics. Boulez had completed his *Le marteau sans maître* and was at work on his Third Piano Sonata and second book of *Structures* for two pianos. Stockhausen's tape masterpiece *Gesang der Jünglinge* was heard for the first time in 1956, as was his *Zeitmasze* for woodwind quintet; his *Gruppen* for three orchestras was in progress. 1956 was also the year of Nono's cantata *Il canto sospeso*.

Faced with this new community – so different from the

Composers' Union of the Hungarian People's Republic, but in its way just as restrictive – Ligeti was for a while silent. He had come west with many ideas (not least the basic ideas for nearly all his major works up to and including the Requiem), but there was much for him to learn, in the electronic studio and beyond: 'On my arrival in Cologne I soaked up things like a sponge: for several months I did nothing but listen to tapes and discs.[1] Apart from the music of the new generation (though not wholly apart), Webern was a crucial discovery, and during the next few years he was to write and lecture much more frequently on Webern than on any other composer, for Webern 'represented a complete abandoning of motivic-thematic thought (something that everyone was looking for, the serialists and the constructivists, like Xenakis). That was exactly what interested me.'[2]

Cologne – and specifically the West German Radio electronic music studio there – had been Ligeti's Eldorado since 1953, when he had first heard about electronic music over the radio: 'When I learned that there existed a procedure allowing the composer to realize his music himself, I was highly interested. That was very important for someone like me, who had no opportunity to hear his works performed. I'd also heard talk of new sonorities, and I was optimistic, like everyone else at that time . . . I wanted to remove myself from the Classic-Romantic tradition, even from Bartók, so I couldn't but be attracted by electronic music (as it was made by Stockhausen and Koenig), and with regard not only to sonority but also form, unfolding, the "flow" of the music. It was a liberation for me – a liberation from this thinking in bars, this measured time.'[3] In the autumn of 1956 he had written to Cologne, and been sent material by the directors of the studio, Herbert Eimert and Stockhausen. He was even able to hear some of Stockhausen's music, under extraordinary circumstances: 'I heard *Gesang der Jünglinge* and *Kontra-Punkte* during the Hungarian revolution; I think that was on 7 November 1956. The artillery was firing, but the western radio stations weren't jammed. People had gone down into cellars; I was alone with my

radio in the apartment.'[4] He contacted Eimert and Stockhausen
again from Vienna. Eimert arranged a bursary for him, and he
stayed for six weeks with the Stockhausens, but, according to his
own account,[5] he learned most from Gottfried Michael Koenig,
Stockhausen's assistant on *Gesang* (and later *Kontakte*), and the
composer of another important Cologne electronic piece of the
time, *Essay* (1957–8). He profited, too, from the presence of
others in the city, including his fellow composers Kagel and
Franco Evangelisti, the poet Hans G. Helms and the critic Heinz-
Klaus Metzger, and he stayed for two years, scraping a living
after the expiry of his four-month scholarship.

His first Cologne composition was *Glissandi* (May–August
1957), a 'finger exercise' in the electronic medium, as he was
later to describe it,[6] and a piece which had little exposure until he
allowed it to appear on disc in the seventies. It was succeeded by
two more electronic pieces, *Pièce électronique no.3* (November
1957–January 1958) and *Artikulation* (January–March 1958), of
which the former was numbered out of sequence because it
remained unrealized after *Artikulation* had been finished. But,
like Stockhausen and Koenig, he was simultaneously composing
outside the studio, working in 1957 on a second version (for
twelve string players with harp, piano, harpsichord and celesta)
of the score that became *Apparitions*. Also that year he produced
a Boulez analysis for the European avant-garde journal, *Die
Reihe*. His intention had been to lay bare some of the secrets of
Le marteau, but this proved too large a task,[7] and so he confined
himself to the opening section from the first book of *Structures*
for two pianos, written six years earlier. His study – one of the
rare classics of musical analysis – is a meticulous and
dispassionate demonstration of how the piece was made. It is,
thereby, a curious, single glimpse of Ligeti as scientist (the tone
contrasts strikingly with the bluster and obfuscation in much of
Die Reihe, and also with the allusiveness, humour and charm
more characteristic of Ligeti's writings and interviews), though
the evidence of discipline, care and a degree of scepticism is

present too, of course, in his music.

But before we follow the course of that music, we should hear a little of the composer's voice as it appeared for the first time in the west, in articles that appeared in the German periodical *Melos* in 1949 and 1950. The first opens with some typically delightful imagery; the second states an aesthetic position with which – leaving aside the political ideology – Ligeti has remained astonishingly consistent, through and into realms of music that even he can hardly then have imagined possible.

1

News from Hungary

We have one Bartók, which is enough. He is great: people abroad see only him, and all the rest are grey, hazy like the houses of a distant city behind the solitary tower. Yet Hungary has a number of important composers. It would be easy for me to write about them if letters were tones, which could replay their music. But this printed matter remains dumb. How can I speak about their works, when you have never heard them?[1]

In his last works Bartók struck an easily understandable note: his language is rigorous, tonal. In the eyes of dogmatic believers in twelve-note music, this may appear reactionary. But if we analyse the works more closely – I am thinking here in the first place of the Concerto for Orchestra and the Third Piano Concerto – we may notice that the phenomenon is not one of a 'return to tonality' but rather of a 'progress to tonality'. Bartók's rigorous, tonal language is not classical. Think just of the beginning of the Adagio of the Third Piano Concerto, where the C major chord suddenly sounds like a new, hitherto unobserved fact of nature . . .

Contemporary Hungarian composers belong to the tonal direction, partly from inner conviction, partly because Bartók has had the biggest influence on them, partly because they feel that the new public needs a simpler, more universally understood music.

Our century's musical revolution has produced very many innovations. If we want to use them to create some clarification, we must throw a lot overboard. For we develop not only by further moulding what is already to hand, but by abandoning many achievements, by limiting means.[2]

2

A New Atmosphere, and
Atmosphères

Ligeti effectively stepped on to the international stage when, on 25 March 1958, West German Radio included in their *Musik der Zeit* series the first presentation of *Artikulation*, the four-track tape piece he had recently completed. To some extent this is a party-line product of the Cologne electronic music studio at the time: what it 'articulates' are bursts of electronic sound masquerading as speech, music thriving on the science of vocal acoustics. But it is special in being also funny and bizarre. Within a duration of under four minutes it mimics a cartoon history of dialogue, screams, howls, bangs, crashes and disasters, all by means of entirely synthetic sounds. *Glissandi* had prepared the way, by exploring where purely sonorous events (glissading tones and noises) turn into representations (very plausibly of, in this case, the conditions of aerial bombardment and radio interference under which the composer heard Stockhausen's *Gesang*), and this sense of the meanings of sounds was evidently conscious and important, as Ligeti explained in his note on *Artikulation*:

> Of course I have no liking for anything expressly illustrative or programmatic, but that does not mean I defend myself against music that suggests associations. On the contrary, sounds and musical contexts continually bring to my mind the feeling of colour, consistency, and visible or even tastable form. And on the other hand, colour, form, material quality and even abstract ideas involuntarily arouse in me musical conceptions. That explains the presence of so

many 'extramamusical' features in my compositions. Sounding planes and masses, which may succeed, penetrate or mingle with one another – floating networks that get torn up or entangled – wet, sticky, gelatinous, fibrous, dry, brittle, granular and compact materials, shreds, curlicues, splinters and traces of every sort – imaginary buildings, labyrinths, inscriptions, texts, dialogues, insect – states, events, processes, blendings, transformations, catastrophes, disintegrations, disappearances – all these are elements of this non-purist music.[1]

This marvellous passage states how far Ligeti was from the avant-garde cult of abstract design, but also how far he was from the traditional idea of expression as a language of melodic-harmonic shape and movement. After all, a gelatinous sound is something very different from a sad tune. Music is, for Ligeti at this juncture, all denotation, not connotation. Sounds and sound processes speak in their own language (the point of *Artikulation*) and do not need a higher language of tonal or serial ordering to make them mean. They are themselves – but in being themselves they are also full of significance.

Such a way of hearing and making sound is conveyed not only in Ligeti's electronic pieces but in the orchestral music he was to write during the next few years – *Apparitions* (1958–9), which had been brought to completion by the time of his remarks above, and *Atmosphères* (1961) – and the projection of 'this non-purist music' was to cause consternation within the avant-garde community at a time when the ties of loyalty were being unloosed also by ideas coming from Cage. More than that, the two orchestral works were to reveal the composer to a much wider public, if to very different degrees, for where *Apparitions* was to remain one of the least frequented zones in his multifarious output, the première of *Atmosphères*, at the 1961 Donaueschingen Festival, was quickly followed by performances on both sides of the Atlantic, and the work is often performed and recorded.

Ligeti's principal innovation in both these scores is the orchestral cluster: the static band of sound in which volume and instrumentation change only slowly or not at all, and in which every note of the chromatic scale within a certain range is sounding. Particularly in *Atmosphères*, the rush of much music of the time is stilled, to bring forward a play of lingering sound, vast and ominous. Not only the stillness but also the sensuality conspicuously contradicts the ideals of Darmstadt and Cologne – though such a reaction was inevitably in the air, as Ligeti has been happy to acknowledge, while stating that he made his way independently. Xenakis had created orchestral clusters by writing for the strings as a body of individuals in his *Metastaseis* (1953–4); Stockhausen was working with comparative motionlessness in *Carré* (1959–60); and the young Penderecki arrived at clusters simultaneously in such works as *Anaklasis* for strings and percussion (1960). Ligeti's distinction was in being at once more extreme, especially in the almost complete abstention from abrupt change he achieved in *Atmosphères*, and more sophisticated, in his precision of detail.

But if the moment of the orchestral cluster had suddenly come, the notion had a long history in Ligeti's imagination, for, as he has recalled, *Apparitions* (and, indeed, much of his later music) can be traced to a childhood experience:

In my early childhood I dreamed once that I could not find a way through to my little bed (which was provided with trellises and provided a perfect sanctuary), because the whole room was filled up by a fine-threaded but dense and extremely complicated web, like the secretion of silk-worms, which spin silk around themselves as pupae to cover the whole inside of the box in which they are cultivated. Beside me there were other beings and objects hanging up in the vast network: moths and beetles of every kind, trying to reach the light around a few barely glimmering candles, and big damp-blotched cushions, their rotten filling tumbling out through tears in the covering. Each movement of the stranded creatures caused a trembling carried throughout the entire system, so that the heavy cushions incessantly lurched hither and thither, and so themselves caused a heaving in the whole. Now and then these movements, acting on one another reciprocally, became so powerful that the net tore in various places and a few beetles unexpectedly were set free, only to be lost again soon in the heaving plaitwork, with a stifling buzz. These events, occurring suddenly here and there, gradually altered the structure of the web, which became ever more twisted: in several places there grew great knots that could never be disentangled; in others caverns, in which a few shreds of the originally connected plaiting floated around like gossamer. The transformations of the system were irreversible; once a state had been passed it could never occur again. There was something inexpressibly sad about this process, the hopelessness of elapsing time and of a past that could never be made good again.[2]

A great deal in this remembered vision chimes with Ligeti's music, and the memory may well have been touched by that music, as much as the music was touched by the memory. The works of his first decade in the west are full of entangled networks, points of clear light, empty spaces, busy objects, and certainly the 'hopelessness of elapsing time' – a hopelessness communicated by music whose continuity allows no image of resolution or birth, and whose slow rate of change mirrors the experience of age and decay.

Ligeti's attempts to realize his boyhood dream in sound began when he was still in Budapest. 'Around 1950, I could *hear* the music I imagined but I did not possess the *technique* of imagining it put on paper. The main trouble was that the possibility had never occurred to me to write music without bars and bar-lines.'[3] During his last year in Budapest he wrote a first version of

Apparitions under the title *Víziók*, but this he found technically unsatisfactory by the new standards he found around him in Cologne, and so in 1957 he began again, planning three movements: the first in the cluster style of the Budapest prototype; the second an extraordinary mobile texture of different repeating figures to be played unaligned by twelve strings, broken only by a second of silence and another second when the prevailing soft dynamic was to be briefly raised to fortissimo,[4] and the third a piece apparently having some connection with the second movement of the Cello Concerto, composed almost a decade later. The definitive *Apparitions* (Ligeti's taste for French titles, he has said, is explained by the inaccessibility of Hungarian and the heaviness of German[5]) has two movements, the first still faithful to the cluster ideal, the second quite new, though it could be seen as an intricately complicated and defined rescheduling of the asynchronous ostinatos.

Apparitions is scored for a large orchestra without oboes, because the work 'has fundamentally an "unreal", ghostly sound, and here the oboes would have been too "concrete".'[6] In terms of structure, the first movement

. . . was influenced by Boulez, Stockhausen and the thinking in Cologne. In this movement there's a repertory of duration elements . . . I worked in this movement a bit like a typesetter making use of little boxes containing letters of the alphabet . . . There was another rule: the proportion of the two big parts of the first movement was based on the golden section, and the subdivisions of these two parts were also made according to the golden section. So the large form (the large building) is constructed after the golden section, the little forms (the bricks) come from the repertory, and there's a region in between where the two procedures meet.[7]

The bricks are generally homogeneous clusters (though there are also cluster glissandos and abrupt soundbites suggestive of

the electronic essays), phonemes which the music whispers or
speaks: Example 1 may suggest how the piece moves to its first
climax through ever more rapid alternation of ever more various
elements. The whole movement is an essay in the drama of sound
blocks, ending with a high cluster maintained by three violins
heard from offstage.

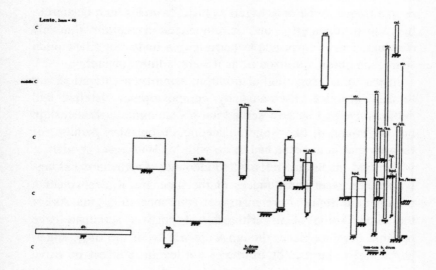

Example 1 Plan of the opening of Apparitions

As in several Bartók works, a slow, introductory movement is
balanced by a faster and more substantial one, in this case an
Agitato which begins with muted and jittery music for orchestral
groups in different metres, and which moves wildly to its end
with brutal stabs and the sound of a tray of crockery being hurled
into a wooden crate lined with metal plates ('possibly wear
protective goggles,' advises the score). The earlier great crisis in
this generally pianissimo movement comes when all forty-six
string players suddenly embark on loud tangled polyphony, each

following a separate trajectory through the chromatic scale (with octave transpositions, so that the predominant intervals are sevenths and ninths). Obviously, there can be no question for the ear of following a particular line, and the chromatic scale is – as Ligeti put it in a contemporary essay, referring here to Nono's *Cori di Didone* – 'simply a regulator to ensure an even distribution of the twelve notes'.[8] As will appear, the chromatic scale has been a frequent visitor to Ligeti's music, from his First Quartet to his Violin Concerto, and it comes as a marker that his chromaticism is in principle harmonic, a matter of filled pitch space; the chromatic scale is, as it were, a linear cluster.

In the same essay, and also within *Apparitions*, Ligeti shows himself at once fascinated by compositional systems, and dubious. He had by now served out his Cologne apprenticeship, but he remained, like Kagel, a sceptic, an outsider, perhaps for reasons that in his case had to do with his Budapest experience, which had made him resistant to ideology. *Apparitions* belongs with other avant-garde pieces of the time, but it also voices a critique: a critique of pretension, of ignorance, of dogma. As for the essay, some of its criticisms of postwar serialism have become commonplace, though were not so at the time. Ligeti particularly regrets, for example, the levelling effect of naïve serialism, the tendency that many small-scale contrasts will create a grey overall image, which he suggests could be avoided by increased attention to matters of large-scale form, incorporating grander contrasts and transitions. He also makes much of a notion of the 'spatialization of the flow of time', by which he seems to mean creating a continuous present – because no promises are being made about the future, as they were in tonal music or in such patently organized music as Webern's – where progression can yet be infinitely variable in speed and substance: not only can time pass more or less quickly, but there can be more or less of it that passes. Finally he casts doubt on the usefulness of aleatory form, which had recently come into vogue with Boulez's Third Piano Sonata and other works in which the

performer has some choice in the ordering of material. 'It seems
to me,' he concludes, 'it would be much more worthwhile to try
and achieve a compositional design of the *process* of change.'

As such a design, *Apparitions* is maybe a shade crude and
over-eager for Ligeti, but it hugely commends his thoughts on
form and texture, especially on how different textures can be
mixed, superposed and interchanged. *Atmosphères* – which grew
out of *Apparitions*, as Ligeti has reported in saying that, in the
second movement of the earlier work, he 'wanted a canon so
dense that it creates a texture, a static tissue, and when I heard the
piece in Cologne in 1960, I heard this tissue which gave me the
starting point for *Atmosphères*'[9] – takes its intentions to a
magnificent apotheosis. Gesture and incident fade, either because
they are absent, leaving simple sustained clusters, or because they
are so manifold as to create only a general impression. In either
case the remnant is a single sounding substance, and the work is
a smooth unfolding of such substances, with only one major
discontinuity, when screeching high piccolos are cut off and
answered by double basses from six octaves below: even here the
feeling is that the music has disappeared over the top of the pitch
spectrum and reappeared at the bottom. Elsewhere, and more
usually, Ligeti achieves the sense of one uninterrupted sound
mass by having his textures overlap with no clear divisions –
entries are often to be imperceptible and extinctions gradual – or
else by having one texture emerge out of another. Also important
to the work's continuity is its lack of percussion instruments,
except for a piano whose strings are brushed at the end.

Atmosphères was the first work Ligeti began after his time in
the Cologne electronic music studio, and the title was one he had
originally chosen for an electronic piece: the project which,
unachieved, became known as *Pièce électronique no.3*. His aim
here had been to create harmonic and subharmonic combinations
of sine tones, swooping from one position in pitch space to
another, and producing resultant difference tones. But there were
technical problems, including the accumulation of background

noise from the mixing of numerous recorded sounds and the interference (in making difference tones) of high frequencies embedded in the tape. Ligeti's means and aims in the orchestral *Atmosphères* are generally quite different, but as a composition of sounds, and of layers of sounds, the work transfers to the orchestral plane an electronic manner of working, and the staggered chordal glissandos of *Pièce électronique no.3* have their equivalent in complex canon, or, to use the composer's own term, 'micropolyphony', which he said he 'would never have been able to develop . . . without the experience of electronic music'.[10]

The outstanding example of micropolyphony in *Atmosphères* is a mirror canon in forty-eight parts, the twenty-eight violins moving in a downward direction while the twenty violas and cellos climb. In each band there is a basic recurring melodic shape: rising semitone then falling tone-semitone-tone (e.g. F♯–G–F–E–D) in the violins, and the inversion of that motif in the violas and cellos. But there is no sustained rhythmic imitation, and the canon is hardly audible as such by virtue of its density and of the *pppp* dynamic level at which most of it goes. The main effect is global, of a cluster covering three and a half octaves (from the C below middle C to F♯ above the treble staff) that is gradually compressed into a minor third. However, where Xenakis or Penderecki might have achieved such an effect with simple glissandos, Ligeti's canon expresses his philosophy of precision. 'I use a way of notating,' he has said, 'that is, one might say, over-precise – a luxury of precision to obtain a result which isn't always very precise, and which can come up with little fluctuations.'[11] Precision is a means, a road from 'the original, general vision' to the equally general performance: 'In between the two, a rational product, so to say, has been manufactured.'[12] But the manufacturing will, of course, leave its traces, spoors of the composer's mind, and in this case they include two elements of high and continuing importance in Ligeti's work: a hint of folk music (in the melodic unit) and complex counterpoint.

'When I think in music,' he has said, 'I think intuitively, but when I compose, I transform that by means of constructions – not as in serial music, or Xenakis's work, but constructions closer to counterpoint, to the isorhythmic motet or to a very learned counterpoint, like Ockeghem's. The counterpoint of Palestrina and Bach, which was taught very exactly in Budapest, left a deep mark on me. I love whatever is constructed.'[13] In mentioning Ockeghem, Ligeti was perhaps thinking of the motet in thirty-six parts that the fifteenth-century composer is reputed to have written, but he went on to suggest that his 'very great interest in the music of Ockeghem' was stimulated by the fact that 'in Ockeghem's music there are imitations half regulated, half free',[14] just as in *Atmosphères*. A certain kind of responsibility is being maintained here. 'Traditional techniques,' as Ligeti has said elsewhere, enable the composer 'to bring the new into shape on the level of the music of the past.'[15] At the same time, lines of contact are kept up – with Ockeghem, with folk music – and the composer's whole sensibility is embodied in a fusion of imagination and memory.

The chromatic cluster – such as that of the forty-eight-part canon, or the stationary one across almost five octaves with which the music opens – is only one of the possibilities of *Atmosphères*. The second big cluster of the piece is reshaped by dynamic changes, which bring forward particular timbres (at first that of the strings) or harmonic colours: the 'white notes' (A–B–C–D–E–F–G) and then the bright ring of horns, flutes and clarinets together on the 'black notes' (A♭–B♭–D♭–E♭–G♭), these diatonic and pentatonic clusters projecting 'a kind of tonal iridescence'.[16] There are also shimmering ribbons produced by many instruments in rapid vibrato, stippled textures in which brief fortissimos are dotted into a continuous pianissimo, and complex wavy patterns of string harmonics in several different metres superposed. The whole piece is a study in what Ligeti in 'Metamorphoses of Musical Form' had called the 'permeability' of musical structures, their capacity to mix with others or stand apart. As the textures arrive, display their variabilities and permeabilities, then leave, they do so as if of themselves. In extreme contrast with *Artikulation*, the music has no voice, and its immense presences imply, rather as in the contemporary paintings of Mark Rothko, an absence – a material absence, in that the music effects the limitation of means for which Ligeti had called in 1950, and a metaphysical one. Of his next important work, the composer was to say that it is 'a structure left empty . . . There is room for melodies in it; everything is ready to receive the thematic elements and motifs; and yet they remain conspicuously absent.'[17]

This next work, written in the winter of 1961–2, was the organ piece *Volumina*, which again works exclusively with clusters, whether chromatic, diatonic or pentatonic, totally immobile or actively figured. However, since Ligeti was now writing for a solo performer (albeit one with an assistant or two to operate the stops) he could save himself a lot of work by indicating the clusters graphically, rather as in Example 1 or, to take a nearer analogy, the plans he had drawn for his electronic compositions: a continuous cluster could simply be indicated by a thick black line, a random texture by a band of squiggles. Some cue for the necessary new performing techniques had come, as Ligeti has acknowledged, from *Konstellationer I* (1958) by the Swedish composer and organist Bengt Hambraeus; *Volumina* was written for Hambraeus's colleague and co-national Karl-Erik Welin, and was the first of many pieces intended for Swedish friends. (In 1961 Ligeti had begun making regular visits to the Stockholm Academy of Music to teach composition: his article 'Über neue Wege in Kompositionsunterricht' includes an account of the skills he wanted to impart – composition with tone-colours, and composition of tone-colours – and of the models he used, together with exercises by his pupils.)

Volumina sounds in part like a transcription of *Atmosphères*: there is again a single disruption when the extreme treble (cluster at the top of the manual, with one-foot stops only) slips over into the extreme bass (cluster at the bottom of the pedalboard, with thirty-two-foot stops only), and again a slow fade at the end, achieved by having the motor switched off while a cluster is maintained, and then by having the performing team blow into small organ pipes by mouth. This results in what the performing instructions describe as 'a "denatured", "out-of-tune" and extremely delicate sound', and the score also allows for weird disintonations at an earlier point, where a weave of activity may be played with the stops half-open. The seemingly paradoxical combination of terms in the composer's own description – 'denatured' and 'delicate' – answers to the effect of his non-traditional tunings, here and in many later works: the effect of estrangement, of discovering a new beauty through gaps in the old. There is a sharp contrast with the work of Kagel, who at just the same time was writing a work for organist and assistants, *Improvisation ajoutée*. The two composers shared a critical view of the musical world around them, but where Kagel, a comic pessimist, brought the organ down to earth, Ligeti, a comic optimist, replaced it in a new heaven.

3

Adventures, and *Aventures*

By now the pattern of Ligeti's life for the next few years was set. In 1959 he had returned to Vienna, following his stay in Cologne, and there he was to remain, apart from his visits to Stockholm. The première of *Apparitions*, at the 1960 festival of the International Society for Contemporary Music, had placed him in the front rank of the avant-garde, which meant that his first performances were gladly claimed by the prestigious German festivals – Donaueschingen (*Atmosphères*, 1961), Bremen (*Volumina*, 1962), Hamburg (*Aventures*, 1963) – and that his music was published by Universal Edition, in common with that of Stockhausen, Boulez, Berio, Kagel and Pousseur.

According to his own account, however, the director of Universal, Alfred Schlee, was reluctant in accepting him into the fold, and he stayed only a short while: *Volumina* began an association with Peters, succeeded in 1967 by Schott. When he was invited to offer a tribute to Schlee on the latter's sixtieth birthday, he therefore responded in kind. *Fragment* (1961) is no fanfare but a curious specimen of music in the far bass register, scored for three double basses, three low wind (double bassoon, bass trombone and double bass tuba), three tuned percussion instruments operating in a low range (harp, celesta and piano), a tamtam used for a single pianissimo, and a large drum. These rumble with the name of the dedicatee, translated into notes as E♭ (German 'Es', therefore 'S'), C, B (German 'H'), E, E. However, Ligeti also satirizes himself, as he has pointed out,[1] for in the space of eleven bars *Fragment* cocks a snook at everything achieved in *Apparitions* and *Atmosphères*. The changeless clusters and the rustling streams are all confined to the dark

cellarage of the audible spectrum, and stasis is carried to a
ridiculous extreme: one 'Schlee' chord has to be held by the
double basses in bottom-most position for between two and four
minutes, broken by a drum thump *sffff*.

Ligeti's capacity for self-mockery is rare among composers,
and endearing. Nor is it by any means limited to this one piece:
in his creative personality, amusement is integrated with
discovery, and to imagine is to have fun. With the completion of
Atmosphères, in July 1961, he had realized a long-cherished
dream, and accomplished the main project of his four and a half
years in the west. He must have felt exhilarated and relieved, and
perhaps also anxious about the path his music might now take:
this was the time for a series of squibs aimed at his own
pretensions and those of his colleagues.

First came his contribution to a symposium on 'The Future of
Music' in August 1961. He said nothing, but used the time and the
blackboard to chalk up remarks addressed to the audience:
'crescendo', 'louder', 'silence' (this in red, and on the occasion
immediately effective). In the same month he wrote *Trois
bagatelles* for David Tudor, whose tour with Cage in 1958–9 had
encouraged European composers to re-approach the piano as an
extension of the player's body – if only 'an enormous artificial
limb',[2] to quote Ligeti's remark on the organ in his note on
Volumina. His bagatelles, though, belong with an older Cage
piece, *4' 33"*, which, extraordinarily, he did not know at the time.
Only one note is played, at the start; the other two bagatelles are
silent, as is the encore piece provided.

Much more serious is the *Poème symphonique* of November
1962. Clearly the idea of a piece for a hundred metronomes is one
that could only have occurred to a composer with a rich sense of
humour or none at all, but this unprecedented ensemble also
supplies the neatest possible resource with which to make
complex layers of different metrical tickings, such as Ligeti had
begun to explore in *Apparitions* and *Atmosphères*, and apparently
also earlier, in the prelude to the unfinished cantata setting

Sándor Weöres's *Istar's Journey in Hell*. Here again, the image goes back to a childhood experience, but this time from the young boy Ligeti's reading rather than his dreams:

> In the works of [Gyula] Krúdy you find again and again a character, a widow whose husband was either a botanist or a meteorologist and has been dead for years . . . One of the stories was about the widow living in a house full of clocks ticking away all the time. The meccanico-type music really originates from reading that story as a five-year-old, on a hot summer afternoon.[3]

As with the tangled, buzzing, insect-haunted network, too, the ticking has continued into later works, as the composer has recognized: 'When I conceived [the *Poème symphonique*], then when I heard it, that gave me many ideas for pieces inspired by machines, as in the Second Quartet, or the Chamber Concerto, or even *Continuum*.'[4] Left out from this list is what might have been his craziest mechanical contraption, had he been able to make it: *Les horloges bienveillantes*, which he planned at the beginning of 1966, and in which the hundred clockwork iterations of the *Poème symphonique* were to have been replaced by snatches of music with different pulses, including Bach motets and French military marches.

Requiring ten metronome operators, the *Poème symphonique* was a brief diversion from work on *Aventures* (May–December 1962), in which he returned to the concerns of *Artikulation*, concerns with how music can imitate language. Stockhausen was working again in the same direction, in *Momente* (1961–4), but *Aventures* is an opera buffa to the broad music drama of that piece. Conceived for three singers and seven instrumentalists, Ligeti's score has no text, only a vast reservoir of sounds with which events may be shaped and expressively underlined. This nonsense language can be adapted to the musical-dramatic situation, and is indeed inseparable from that situation, as may be suggested by an excerpt from the baritone's scena (see Example 2), where the open syllables help to indicate a rather drunken exhibitionism undercut by muttering self-doubt.

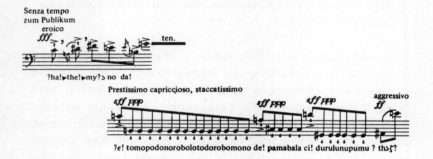

Example 2 From Aventures

But this is only one of the work's adventures. With the two other singers a coloratura soprano and a contralto, many different moods and relationships can be suggested, and the function of the instrumentalists is not only to echo, support and comment but also at times to lead the way. The different atmospheres of the piece include a crazy 'Conversation' for the three singers alone, an ominous echo where a double bass holds on to a very low note, a chattering hubbub interrupted by isolated cries from singers and players, and a final contralto solo in which, by contrast with the baritone's moment quoted above, isolation brings not bravura but a sense of lonely waiting. As Ligeti has put it, the work is 'a kind of "opera" with the unfolding adventures of imaginary characters on an imaginary stage.'[5] 'The form,' he has explained,

> . . . is very complicated: five parallel streams of events – as it were, five 'stories' – that diverge from one another. The form arises from the combining and intertwining of these streams. Each stream consists of a number of separated

episodes (seven to eleven per stream), and each episode has its own very distinctive expressive character (e.g. mystical, idyllic, nostalgic, funereal, redeemed, excited, ironic, erotic, becalmed, humorous, hypocritical, cold, indifferent, triumphant, pathetic, stupid, hysterical, emotional, startled, fiery, exalted, anxious, unrestrained, mannered-ornamental, malicious, etc., etc.).[6]

The description is fair. *Aventures* is the first of many Ligeti pieces that have something of a strip-cartoon character, parading sharply focused images of human encounters and mental states, using the medium vividly, exaggerating expression but also framing it. After two works in which the rule had been gradual change, *Atmosphères* and *Volumina*, Ligeti was now abruptly juxtaposing things incompatible and contradictory – including echoes from his earlier territory. *Aventures* starts in a tight cluster around middle C, and is visited thereafter by other shadows of the stasis of *Atmosphères*, as well as by ideas that come straight from the more disrupted *Apparitions* (stamping low clusters in the harpsichord, for instance, or the plain chromatic scale made miraculously strange, surrounded by whispers and noises in the 'Action dramatique' towards the end of the piece). As a comic-dramatic parade of voices and voicings, the work relates more thoroughly to *Artikulation*, like which it shares in the contemporary exploration of vocal sound and at the same time debunks any grandiloquent pretension.

By its nature *Aventures* implies serial continuation, and in 1965, having completed his Requiem, Ligeti added a further pair of movements as *Nouvelles aventures*. Apparently he had intended *Aventures* to have two movements, the second concluding where the first had begun: *Nouvelles aventures* supplies this episode, though not as an ending (it comes near the end of the new work's first movement), and includes other material drafted in 1962, such as the mechanical section 'Les horloges démoniaques'.[7] Yet the new adventures are different from the old. 'There are,' Ligeti wrote, 'still more human feelings than in *Aventures*, but the most intense emotions and expressions are in a way dissected and laid out, so that they become completely cool.'⁸ *Nouvelles aventures* is also more intricately composed, faster in pace, and odder, the episodes more compact, more elusive, and sometimes perhaps touched by the composer's intervening work on the Requiem: a notable instance is the chorale in two parts with octave transpositions and soft hazardous sonorities (low piccolo and low stopped horn, double-bass harmonics). *Nouvelles aventures* raises and amplifies *Aventures* by enlarging its dimensions and its scope.

In 1966 Ligeti tried to give the double composition still more solidity by binding it round with a stage scenario, which, with pauses and scene changes, would run for forty minutes. Extravagant and bizarre music meets an extravagant and bizarre staging. For example, the baritone solo quoted above (Example 2) takes place with the following business as Ligeti sets it out in the libretto:

The Olympic Runner (male dancer) bursts on to the stage, breathless, exhausted, coming from the opposite side from the Golem. In one hand he carries a burning torch, in the other a scroll. On his arrival the preceding 'Conversation' stops silent, and the baritone hides himself behind an invisible three-person-wide Spanish screen. (This screen, dazzling white like the background, stands there unremarked from the beginning of the scene and must not contrast with the background, so that, as the baritone and his double disappear, come out and disappear again, one has the impression that the people in question are invisible behind the screen, then visible again, and so on. The camouflaging of the screen can be effected by means of shadowless lighting.) The soprano and the contralto are silenced together and frozen in their last positions, as if a film has stopped. The baritone sings the first phrase of the bar unseen behind the screen; the Olympic Runner accompanies the phrase with mime and gesture, as if he were singing, as if he were pronouncing an extremely important message, fatal to all present. At the end of the phrase (which he seems to fling out heroically, totally exhausted, with all that remains to him) he suddenly catches sight of the Golem: at the same moment he collapses, and falls lifeless to the ground, while his torch goes out and his scroll (with the unknown, so important message) rolls away – nobody will bother with it again.

And so on. All this covers only one phrase, and though Ligeti's libretto for *Aventures* and *Nouvelles aventures* is not always as detailed, it is nearly always as crazy. However, by finding explanations for how the singers and instrumentalists behave, the scenic version undermines both the purity and the dramatic effectiveness of the original pieces. The dramatis personae of *Aventures* and *Nouvelles aventures* are not characters but singers, which is why their responses have to be vocal and generally exaggerated; their milieu is the concert stage, which is enough to account for the alienation and aloneness they seem to feel through much of the proceedings. Like Winnie in Beckett's contemporary play *Happy Days* (1961), they are terrified by silence and emptiness, and so they find little activities to fill up their time. They tell each other stories; they exchange confidences; they play games. And because they are musicians, their narratives are operatic and their pastimes musical. Because, too, they are human, their ploys are only temporarily convincing – to themselves or to us. Either they rush from one episode straight into another, or else the enemy silence descends and they 'remain as if turned to stone', as the common stage direction has it. They are alive only when they are making a noise: silence alarms and embarrasses them, and they stop – or else silence simply turns them off, as if they were machines, toys. To be immured in silence, to be stilled, is to be dead. At one point, though, they are allowed to expect something from beyond silence, and to have their expectation gratified. Towards the end of the first movement of *Nouvelles aventures* the contralto and baritone sing a unison E♭, and then all three singers 'wait, rigid and listening, for an echo from the far distance'. When it comes, as a soft horn tone, they are pleased; when it is repeated, by other instruments, they are astonished.

This is, in a very characteristically Ligetian manner, both touching and comic. The three singers on stage are, as characters, three people alone in their little universe, unaware of their accompanying instrumentalists (so that a horn sound can be a voice from the unknown) and unaware of their audience: they lack the confident reciprocity of performers within a shared tradition, and in that lack – which is actualized in a different way by their lack of words – they place themselves at a moment of crisis in western musical culture. But their ignorance is also the ignorance of children – the ignorance and the innocence, as they carry on their pre-verbal babble. And of course they give us an image of ourselves: as children, as alone, as engaging in meaningless activities (such as music) in order to protect ourselves from nothingness, as trusting with frail hope in something beyond.

In 1966, the year after *Nouvelles aventures*, Ligeti's main achievement was his Cello Concerto, which he described at an early point in the process of composition as 'a kind of "*Aventures* without words", or indeed with words that the cello "speaks".'[9] The final work, in its pathos, humour and strangeness, is true to this conception – though so too is a very great deal else he has written, from *Apparitions* onwards. Indeed, one of the most distinctive features of his output is the *Aventures* principle: that music has words (expressive gestures) but no language, and that this situation is at once tragic and delightful. What changed as the Cello Concerto went ahead, though, was the form. Ligeti had begun with the idea of a sequence of eighteen episodes, but one of these grew to become a movement by itself, the first, and the others came to infiltrate one another in a chase of musical characters. This second movement, Ligeti reported,

> could be regarded formally as a set of variations, except that they aren't variations so much as a steady unfolding (like a big development in which one doesn't know which musical ideas will really be 'developed'). During this unfolding, apparently alien inserts are brought in by means of the 'window technique,' but the windows subsequently appear, as the form progresses, not as alien material but as 'windows giving onto the same landscape'. At the end one doesn't know what was window and what not-window; besides, within the windows there are 'smaller' windows, and so on.[10]

Some of the smaller windows are almost direct transcriptions of elements from *Aventures* or *Nouvelles aventures*: another frantic hocket, more instances of musical clockwork in which instruments lend their staccato ticks (tics) to an effect of mechanical purposelessness, more tremulations, more bursts of virtuosity. However, the movement also has connections with a more immediate predecessor: the first movement of the concerto. This begins with an E on the cello, gradually brought into consciousness; the initial marking is *pppppppp*, 'entry inaudible, as if coming out of nothing'. Ligeti has remarked how 'several of my works . . . start with a very simple pattern . . . [which] takes the place, and quite intentionally, of thematic development'.[11] However, this analogy does not provide the whole story, for the unnoticed arrival (and departure) of such a work as the Cello Concerto joins it seamlessly into silence; it is not an object in time, which we aurally peruse, but a state through which we pass – a state which may, nevertheless, offer up objects to us, like the moments of machinery or gushes of bravado: Ligeti himself has conveyed the difference in saying how for him structure is 'conceived not as an edifice one builds, but rather as a slightly liquid mass'.[12] As the cello's E, in this case, continues, so it gets louder, is picked up by other instruments, and becomes dirtied with harmonics; then the F above is added, followed by more neighbour notes to make a small chromatic cluster, which is abruptly replaced by the magical sound of a previously unheard pitch, B♭, sounding across five octaves on calm, vibratoless strings. This image too is sullied, until an emphatic chord from the harp cuts off everything except for the soloist and the double bass, the former rising through high harmonics on the A string over an abyss reaching down almost six octaves. 'The end of the first movement of the Cello Concerto made me think of tightrope-walking . . . Seeking the limits of instrumental and vocal possibility attracted me. I wanted this dangerous kind of expression, this demoniac aspect.'[13]

The second movement resembles the first in that rush and stasis are different kinds of continuity. Except where windows open and close suddenly, the rapid musical activities here emerge from and merge back into one another, and, as Ligeti has noted, the ending is 'a figured variant'[14] of the first movement's, with the perilous, ultimately disintegrating harmonic replaced by a 'whisper cadenza' that loses itself in tiny noises and silences. The idea of two movements as opposite equals, or alter egos, goes back to *Apparitions* and to Bartók, but the particular notion of 'rhyming' movements by bringing them to close at similar points is more peculiarly Ligeti's, and was to recur in much of his later music. Another typical feature found in the Cello Concerto is the festooning of the printed music with explanatory footnotes, testifying to his ultra-precision and to his keen sense of a sound's gesture and quality. Ligeti suggested at the time that this was his best piece,[15] and one can understand why he might have thought so. It contains more of his musical personality than anything he had composed hitherto – utter stasis, utter derangement, lost memories (the doleful falling minor second), new inventions – and yet everything about it is crisp, neat and compact. Much more, however, lay in the future.

4

Requiem

First, though, we must look back again. The gap between *Aventures* and *Nouvelles aventures* was not empty but filled by the Requiem, which Ligeti began in the spring of 1963 and finished in January 1965. It was a project of long standing, if a slightly curious one on the part of a Jewish composer: Ligeti has said that what attracted him to the Requiem text was the sequence 'Dies irae' (Day of Wrath), with its terrible vision of the Last Judgement coming with fire and trumpets, and with its brutal, insistent metre, each stanza having three short rhyming lines. All human death is there, but expressed in a manner at once grandiose and naïve, monitory and hysterical, alarming and comic. Or at least so it appears in Ligeti's setting, which has the retrospective effect of making one a little uncertain about whether earlier versions by Mozart, Berlioz and Verdi can be taken quite straight – though, according to Ligeti, these composers were less in his mind than Pérotin and Machaut.[1]

The connection with Pérotin goes back to his first attempt at a Requiem.

The first idea that I worked out, while I was a student at the Academy, was to have a chorus accompanied by harps and percussion, practically a Requiem with cuckoo accompaniment – but I meant it as a serious work, not as a joke. The idea probably came from something I had heard during the war, or perhaps just after the war. János Hammerschlag . . . for a performance of a work by Pérotin . . . duplicated the human voice with all kinds of percussion: a glockenspiel, as well as all kinds of bells. Pérotin was transformed into a mixture of church music and fairground music.[2]

Then in the early fifties he began a new setting in 'a kind of pentatonic serialism.'³ But before he could achieve his Requiem he perhaps needed to explore and develop the necessary means: the bizarre juxtapositions and accumulations of *Apparitions*, the clusters and micropolyphonic clouds of *Atmosphères*, the human comedy of *Aventures*.

To open the definitive work, the 'Introitus' begins very slowly and quietly in the extreme bass register, the Latin ('Rest eternal grant unto them, O Lord: and may light perpetual shine upon them') intoned by a choir of basses in four parts, accompanied by the cavernous lowest instruments of the orchestra: trombones, double bass trombone, horns, double bass tuba, bass and double bass clarinets, double bassoon, double basses. The mention of perpetual light 'evoked in me essential images of colour: eight-note chords played on six double basses and two cellos, all of them sounding fairly low harmonics. This combination produces a glass translucence, which also gives the effect of 'dark' light'.⁴ The feeling is enormously solemn and awe-inspiring, and also alien, like that of the dedication to death in Egyptian funerary art. But it is also, in a very Ligetian paradox, rather absurd. For example, during this first section of the 'Introitus' the basses wander within a narrow compass from E♯ to A at the bottom of the bass staff, except at the word 'Domine', for which two soloists plunge to C♯ and D♯: a term of exaltation is given the furthest possible abasement. Very slowly, then, the black cloud begins to rise. Contraltos and tenors enter, albeit in their lowest registers and similarly jostling within narrow pitch bands. After them the two soloists, mezzo and soprano, arrive, followed by the choral mezzos and sopranos, while the orchestra grows brighter with the inclusion of flutes, clarinets, trumpet and upper strings.

The ensuing 'Kyrie' is the most overwhelmingly impressive product of Ligeti's cluster style. It is more measured than *Atmosphères*, and more monumental, keeping the introit's division of the choir into five four-part sections in order to create a quasi-fugue whose lines are four-part micropolyphonic canons.

György Ligeti

Example 3 shows the start, and provides a typical instance of
Ligeti's micropolyphony, where canons at the unison create
swarms that can move steadily in pace (through changes in the
rhythmic unit) and register. Two four-part braids are beginning
here; there will be a total of twenty-three, twelve of them setting
the words 'Kyrie eleison' and eleven 'Christe eleison'. Right
through the movement, the melodic lines take the form of a sort
of Brownian motion, a jostling in small intervals that, with the
rhythmic displacement between parts, contributes to the effect of
worried discontent. Crystal clarity is not the aim. 'The singers
cannot help making mistakes in the intonation, which produces a
kind of microtonality, dirty patches; and these dirty patches are
very important.'[5] Hence the effect of a haze and a murmuring
hubbub. Instead of an ordered community moving with mutual
respect along the lines of a canon, we are presented with a mob.

Yet through this foggy material, like shafts of light in different colours, come octaves or unisons sounded by the orchestra to celebrate the opening pitch of each braid as it starts, octaves or unisons that mark out in giant strides the stepwise movement simultaneously up and down the chromatic scale from the first B♭ to the final B♭. Since the instruments are otherwise doubling the voices, these beams of sound stand out prominently. The effect is momentous, especially when the music is at its busiest, as it is towards the end of each half of the movement, each coming to a climax when the choral sopranos hit high B♭.

The third movement, 'De die judicii sequentia' (Sequence of Judgement Day, i.e. 'Dies irae'), could be regarded as *Aventures* gone oratorical. The 'Day of Wrath' has come, and Ligeti launches it with a hectic energy and chopped violence in complete contrast with the music of continuity that has reigned hitherto. 'In the "Dies irae" I saw the sequence as a colourful picture-book, with new images conjured up all the time, in every third line. Here I definitely wanted to paint pictures in music.'[6] Voices and instruments sound together in mechanical staccato patterns that tumble over one another, triplets and quintuplets conflicting with the fast semiquaver pulse, the dynamic aggressively fortissimo. No sooner have they started than they stop, as if startled by their own emphatic insistence. Then the deathcart is set rolling again, briefly, before another 'picture in music' takes over. Two stanzas have been rattled off, and we are left with a low B♭ in horns and bassoons, cut off by the mezzo soloist stretching words over enormous intervals and singing at first in long notes. 'Wondrous sound the trumpet flingeth,' she declaims, and trumpets and trombones duly fling out a G♭ in unison with her. But the end of her phrase is a spurt of semiquavers, *sfff*, which prompts a mad rush from the same instruments, squashed by a dry tamtam stroke. There is something crazily comic in this passage. The injunction to the singer – 'suddenly: very menacing, very vehement' – invites her to protest too much, and the galloping collapse of the brass comes

Example 3 Opening of the 'Kyrie' of the Requiem

like a ripple of mockery, on which the percussionist peevishly stamps his foot. One is reminded – especially given the vocal style – of Ligeti's description of the songs and canons of Webern's middle period as 'so overcharged that in effect they turn completely cold'.[7] One is reminded too of painters Ligeti admires, Breughel and Bosch, whose visions of the vanity of human existence produced monsters of disquieting comedy.

The first mention of death, at the beginning of the fourth stanza, brings another gargoyle: the whole choir together in low, almost spoken incantation, ticking over like a machine running out of steam. (The same style will recur for the eighth stanza, 'King of Majesty', the first appeal for mercy.) Later there are rapturous duets for the women soloists, and finally some return of the choral clouds from the 'Kyrie' as the portrait of Doomsday turns decisively into a prayer for personal redemption. Much of the music is stark, even when scored for enormous forces, since the rhythms tend to be hard-edged, the phrases short, the structure lapidary. Yet these are the means too, again, of the comic strip; the undercurrent of ridiculousness remains, and with it the closeness to *Aventures* and *Nouvelles aventures*. Many gestures are shared: the hocketing lines that swing crazily from one voice to another, the high male falsetto as an expression of forcefulness gone over the top, the blackly echoing low cluster in the harpsichord. And of course the connection works both ways. The Requiem is as much a musical joke as *Aventures* and *Nouvelles aventures* are meditations on the last things. Frivolity edges over into profundity, as in *Atmosphères* the piccolos edge over into the double basses; all that is missing is the huge middle ground we thought was normality.

Unlike those earlier composers who parcelled the 'Dies irae' up into a succession of arias or choruses, Ligeti goes right through the text until he has just two stanzas left for his fourth and final movement, the 'Lacrimosa'. It was in setting this passage that Mozart died, and in Ligeti's setting there is a sense that most of the world has passed away. Where in the previous movement he has sported with two soloists, two choirs (of which the larger is used only in this part of the work) and a large orchestra, in the finale he writes for the soloists only, with an orchestra thinned to diaphany. Once more the essential method is that of micropolyphony, but now generally in just two parts (with octave doublings), so that intervals resound with a new luminosity especially in the context of what has gone before. And the orchestra bathes the music with octaves, or with a high chord of fourths and fifths.

This is something new in Ligeti's music, as he recognized. And something new is needed. We have just been through the Last Judgement: things cannot be the same again. The 'Lacrimosa' hints at a transfigured survival, but only hints, for it is desperately uncertain – as uncertain as are its hollow harmonies, threadbare textures and slow speed. Too much has been lost for us to move with anything but extreme caution. The point is philosophical, in that the Requiem is about death; it is historical, in that Ligeti had twice experienced the 'Day of Wrath' visiting his native Hungary, during the Nazi occupation and in the years of Stalinist terror; and it is musical, in that the work moves towards a reconsideration of what the cluster style had almost obliterated: harmony.

The evidence of Ligeti's recollections, at least, is that his reinvention of a basic musical vocabulary was quite conscious. In *Atmosphères*: 'I decidedly wanted to eliminate pitches . . . Later, beginning with the Requiem, I began to re-use pitches.'[8] Then: 'When I finished the Requiem I became aware that I had to distance myself from clusters . . . In the last movement of the Requiem (the Lacrimosa) I made use of very clear intervals, and that led me to a music like that of *Lux aeterna* the next year.'[9] The latter piece, setting a further passage from the Latin mass for the dead (though the words are virtually obliterated in performance, thanks to the slow speed and the overlappings of voices) and completed just before the Cello Concerto, was commissioned by Clytus Gottwald for his Schola Cantorum of Stuttgart. This was a professional group – the expert ensemble for new unaccompanied choral music – and Ligeti could now expect finer tuning than in the case of the Requiem. Once again the technique is that of spreading chromatic micropolyphony, starting out from a middle F intoned by sopranos and contraltos (the first male voice enters only at the end of the twenty-fourth bar, and a little later the texture becomes totally male for a similar span), but the clusters periodically condense into simpler harmonies, and, as Ligeti has pointed out, much of the music floats in, towards and around a chord made up of a minor third topped by a major second, such as G–B♭–C, which comes at the point near the middle of the piece where the women re-enter and the words are 'Requiem aeternam'.

To this chord, placed inside octave Gs, are added other notes, starting with F♯, A and E, which in Ligeti's terms begin to complete an 'acoustic scale' – though since the 'pillar' (his term) is G, one could regard the mode compressed here as Dorian with a raised seventh (G–A–B♭–C–[D]–E–F♯–G). Precise definition is impossible, because what concerns us is, once again, no more than a trace of the composer's background in folk music and in Bartók, whose 'chromatic tonality' he has cited as a definite influence on him: 'There are tonal centres, but the language is chromatic: I think that can be seen very clearly in Bartók's Second Quartet.'[10] The passage also offers clear evidence of Ligeti's aural sensitivity. According to his own account, the chord 'gives, as it transforms itself, a metallic sonority coming from the acoustic scale, but a little jumbled . . . The choir itself isn't metallic, but it's as if you had a bell, or something like that . . . I synthesize a sort of imaginary bell with human voices.'[11]

This is the sort of harmony – hesitant and unstable – that *Lux aeterna* recovers out of the chaos of clusters and clouds, at the end of a suite of Requiems that must also be allowed to include *Atmosphères*, which Ligeti inscribed to the memory of an older Hungarian composer who had left his country, Mátyás Seiber (1905–60). Once asked about the Requiem-like nature of that piece, Ligeti replied that he would prefer not to be drawn about 'such a personal aspect of composition'. Nevertheless, the luminous chords that begin to shine in the 'Lacrimosa' and *Lux aeterna* promise a kind of resurrection.

5

Harmonies

Lux aeterna was, like *Apparitions*, a turning point in Ligeti's music, and like *Apparitions* it was followed by a big orchestral piece dispensing with percussion in order to create a broad sound continuum: *Lontano*, completed in May 1967, is music revisiting the orchestra of *Atmosphères*, only with lighter brass and no brushed piano. Between *Lux aeterna* and this new work had come the Cello Concerto, whose first movement is another instance of cloud music tinted with definite harmonic colours. *Lontano*, however, marks the full assumption of the new style, and – resembling *Atmosphères* also in this – it moves with majestic slowness through a newly discovered world.

The title, meaning 'distant' suggests the musical use of the term to indicate sounds that appear to come from far away or that actually are played by instruments offstage, as in Beethoven's third *Leonore* overture or Mahler's Second Symphony – or indeed Ligeti's *Apparitions*. In *Lontano* all the instruments are on the platform, but there are sensations of distance on several levels. Like *Atmosphères* and the first movement of the Cello Concerto, the piece begins very quietly and ends with a prolonged fade, giving the impression that it arrives from far away and slowly departs, as if, in Ligeti's own words, opening and closing 'a window on long-submerged dream-worlds of childhood'.[1] Beyond that, still more than in *Atmosphères*, there is a feeling of orchestral space, perhaps with quiet sustained chords in the background and more definite figures nearer at hand, and Ligeti's new harmonic practice contributes to such illusions: a chime of octaves, for instance, sounds closer than a more complex chord (though it may evoke a greater distance through time, back to the imagined childhood of music). Qualities of distance and nearness will depend too on the loudness of events, their register (high and low notes tending to sound further away), their orchestration (the brass, for instance, having more presence than the strings), the seating of the orchestra (the initial A♭, for instance, sounding from flutes and cellos, and therefore both far and near) and fine points of tuning. The exact shade a violinist gives to a particular note will hang on the melodic and harmonic context; a plain fifth in the strings will tend to be played in just intonation rather than equal temperament. All these effects might normally be negligible flickers, but in *Lontano*, where processes of change are so much decelerated, they begin to become significant, and to help create the music's essential impalpability and mystery.

The work begins almost as a transposition of *Lux aeterna* up a minor third; it develops the same melody, and does so again through canons, though on a more elaborate scale.[2] It is, Ligeti has said, 'a parody of *Lux aeterna*'[3] in the Renaissance sense. There are three broad stages to the piece, of which the first begins with the drawing near of A♭ as the note is taken up by clarinets, bassoons and horns; then the unison starts to dissolve, as in *Lux aeterna*, with the addition of nearby notes. (Apparently, it is no more than a coincidence that the original note, in German 'As', provides a musical monogram for Arnold Schoenberg, whose study in static orchestral chords, the third of his Five Pieces op.16, provided Ligeti with an ancestral voice resembling his own.) By the time the opening tone has swivelled into G♯, it has become just one component in a complex chord which spreads and thins in a glistening sharp-flavoured texture developed largely in the strings. There is another switch into the flat region, and then a new focus becomes ever more dominant as C starts to sound in treble-register octaves throughout the orchestra. The highest C remains as a harmonic in two violins throughout what can be regarded as a transitional passage, this belatedly introducing two notes that have been neglected until now, D and F. (Here again Ligeti generally works with modal rather than chromatic clusters.) As at the end of the first movement of the

Cello Concerto, there is the illusion of space within the music, for the continuing high C hovers nearly six octaves above the D♭ infiltrated by tuba, double bassoon and double bass. The second main section begins with another simple sound, that of the tritone E–B♭ played in octaves by the strings, and there is another process of deliquescence and reformation coming to rest on a unison bass F. The final phase starts at once from the fourth D–G in harmonics on cellos and basses, and reaches up to high D♯s, which evaporate to leave the piece drawing away in the low register.

With the clear harmonies that glow and fade across its huge surfaces (another example is the G–B♭–C chord again, in the middle section), *Lontano* achieves something spectacularly different from its predecessor: '*Atmosphères* was to a large extent grey: it was colourful in the sense of tone-colour, but harmonically grey. In *Lontano*, on the other hand, both tone-colour and harmony are colourful.'[4] This is not harmony, though, in any traditional sense: the chords do not underpin the music, but rather the music underpins the chords, which could imaginably be quite different. Goals like the high C in the first third of the work only emerge as goals once the music has begun to reach them, and there is no logic of harmonic connection. Ligeti has spoken of the 'remarkably soft crystal formations'[5] in the music, of the harmonic crystals that dissolve and precipitate, sometimes little by little, sometimes all at once and scintillant.

He had got to this point by a double negation:

> The abolition of non-harmony leads back to harmony. But this newly evolved harmony is not the same as the former harmony – the historical process is irreversible, recurring aspects notwithstanding . . . In *Lontano* intervallic structures are subjected to a continual transformation, similar to the transformation of tone colours in *Atmosphères*. The intervals as such are the same as in earlier music, but they are handled in a fundamentally different way: with the sounds of a dead language a new language is being evolved.[6]

So it is: *Lontano* once again reinvents orchestral sound. Yet the tug of the past is powerfully felt, and adds another layer to the significance of the title, for *Lontano* is a backward gaze at the orchestral sumptuousness of the late Romantic period – at the rich octave-doubled textures of that time and at momentary effects, such as the soft, warm entry of horns near the end, which Ligeti himself feels to allude to the coda in the slow movement of Bruckner's Eighth Symphony.[7]

As it was after *Atmosphères*, Ligeti's next step was to transpose a newly acquired technique from the orchestra to the organ. *Harmonies*, the first of a pair of studies, was composed two months after *Lontano* for the Hamburg organist Gerd Zacher, who had been among the early assailants on *Volumina* and had asked for a new piece. As in *Volumina*, the notation is greatly simplified. No composer of organ music can predict what stops will be available, or quite what effect they will have, and so such care as Ligeti brings to the composition of orchestral textures would be in vain. *Harmonies* offers just a simple succession of chords, changing one note at a time (usually by semitone movement), and finally thinning out the ten-note assemblies that have been the rule. Even this rudimentary notation is suspect, and much more so than in the case of *Atmosphères* or *Lontano*, with their anticipated exquisite irregularities of tuning, for Ligeti's directions ask for 'greatly reduced wind pressure ("artificial consumptiveness")' to produce 'pale, strange, "vitiated" tone colours' and disintonations, as briefly in *Volumina*, harmonies that are 'tainted'. There is an irony here, though again a kindlier irony than Kagel's; the king of instruments is being dethroned, but there is something wonderful about the dethronement, positive about the exploration of microtones. It is as if the written text were being placed at the bottom of a water tank, and seen through unpremeditated ripples. Ligeti, otherwise hostile to the sixties vogue for chance, lets his music be affected by the fortuitous.

At this point, with his interests centred in slow drift, he was asked to write a piece for an instrument of exactly opposite properties: the harpsichord. However, he realized that he could achieve the 'usual Ligeti effect' by capitalizing on the harpsichord's high speed: small groups of notes, repeated over and over, would be perceived as harmonies, could be made to glide and shift by changing the notes, and would gain a useful cloudiness from the successive nature of the attacks. Hence *Continuum*. This is something very different from the harpsichord writing in *Apparitions*, *Aventures* and the Requiem, where chilly resonances in the bass are most characteristic. *Continuum* busies itself mostly in the middle register, as fast as possible, with both hands engaged in repeating patterns in the manner of finger exercises: a two-manual instrument makes it possible for the hands to be locked together in the same pitch space. 'It suddenly came to me,' Ligeti has remarked, 'that a harpsichord was really like some strange machine.'⁸ And so he invented the piece 'entirely from the harpsichord's possibilities', among them 'extreme speed, extreme lightness of attack', with the speed assisted by the fact that 'the placement of the hands is always the same, only the stretch changes. Two hands are composed, so to speak, as objects in movement.'⁹

The composer's charity allows these objects to scan simpler chords than those of *Harmonies*. The piece starts out from a minor third, G–B♭, in both hands, to which it first adds the F a major second below, so creating an inversion of the chord important to both *Lux aeterna* and *Lontano*. From here the fingers creep out to cover all the notes within the tritone F–C♭, after which notes are successively dropped to leave the major second F♯–G♯, which then gains the D♯ below to form a new version of the 'Ligeti chord'. The next step is a gradual filling-in to produce a fragment of the C♯ major scale (suddenly the piece sounds like a practice exercise), which slowly changes itself before the first quick switch, to a B major triad. Ligeti is now confident enough of his crystallization-dissolution technique to embrace frankly tonal harmonies, and with the addition of its seventh, then its sixth, the B major chord slowly subsides into the tonal uncertainty (anxiety, one might say) more typical of the piece. From this point the hands separate, then the bass register is lost, and finally the harmony reaches its furthest attenuation as just a high F♭ is left in insistent iteration, like a maddened insect.

One striking and profitable discovery Ligeti made in *Continuum* was that of what one might call 'resultant rhythm' produced by the interference of separate but similar parts. As Ligeti has put it: 'The actual rhythm of the piece is a pulsation that emerges from the distribution of the notes, from the frequency of their repetitions.'[10] Example 4 shows an instance from early in the composition, where what sticks out particularly is the irregular beating of Fs produced by the overlapping of non-aligned and changing ostinatos (a rhythm that could be represented as: ./..//././/.../...//..//.././/..../). Ligeti was to use the same technique in the second movement of the Double Concerto and the first movement of the Chamber Concerto, and then, with far greater sophistication, in his music of the eighties and nineties.

Example 4 From Continuum

Among the prototypes for *Continuum* he has mentioned Bach's C minor prelude, Chopin's Etudes and Debussy's 'Feux d'artifice',[11] but not the repetitive music that had recently got under way across the Atlantic, because that movement – represented by Terry Riley's *Keyboard Studies* (1963) and Steve Reich's *Piano Phase* (1967), of which the latter also exploits slipping ostinatos and resultant rhythms – was as yet unknown in Europe. (One has to blame the zeitgeist again for the coincidence.) Ligeti, however, was far from unknown in the United States, where in the year of *Continuum*, 1968, Stanley Kubrick was putting *Atmosphères*, the 'Kyrie' of the Requiem and *Lux aeterna* into the company of the Strausses, Johann II and Richard, in the score of his film *2001*. This unsolicited borrowing surely increased awareness of his music, if of a kind of music he was no longer writing.

He had moved on, rather, to chamber formations – string quartet, wind quintet, string ensemble – but then in July 1969 came a direct successor to *Continuum* in the second organ study, *Coulée* ('Flow'), where again the musical substance consists of prestissimo repeating figures on two equal manuals. Another feature shared by these two manic keyboard pieces, in contrast with the slow final fades of other works, is the instruction to 'stop suddenly, as though torn off' – words that had been used in *Aventures* and *Nouvelles aventures* to interrupt some of the musical mechanisms, and that would recur frequently on Ligeti's scores; the effect, of course, is the same as that of a fade, to suggest that there is no real ending. Finally, both *Continuum* and *Coulée* welcome the fortuitous noises their instruments produce. The sound of the harpsichord's action is likely to come into its own under the last high tremolo of *Continuum*, and the composer's instructions for *Coulée* ask that the striking of the keys be audible and have 'the effect of a very fast time grid'. Machine music is by no means disturbed by aural evidence of its mechanical source.

6

Four and Five

By the time of *Continuum* Ligeti had been in the west for eleven years, and had completed as many works, not counting the electronic pieces and the satires of 1961–2. But all those works had been for large forces or a solo keyboard player: the whole middleground of music had been left out (though chamber music had been central to Ligeti's activity in Hungary). It was time for a change – especially for a composer eager to find new challenges, as he remarked of himself around this time: 'I could not write again today anything like, for example, my orchestral pieces of a few years ago, *Apparitions* and *Atmosphères*. I want to go further within my own kind of composition . . . By that I don't at all mean development, but simply different new aspects or for me new solutions to compositional problems.'[1] He may also have wanted to consolidate, to bring together the disparate kinds of music he had set in motion. The string quartet offered both a new sphere (for so much had happened during the fourteen years since he had last written for this medium) and the invitation to a multi-movement integration of diversities, which could include the slowly disturbed unison of *Lontano* (and on the same note, though spelled as G♯, opening the second movement), the demented machine music of *Aventures*, *Nouvelles aventures* and the Cello Concerto (third movement) and the flowing patterns of *Continuum* (fifth movement particularly).

As the composer has put it:

I wanted to realize one and the same musical . . . concept in the five movements of the string quartet, and so relate them to one another . . . In the first movement the structure is largely broken up, as in the Requiem or in *Aventures*: one could almost describe it as an instrumental variant of these works. In the second movement everything is reduced to very slow motion . . . The third movement is a pizzicato piece: this is possibly the clearest allusion to Bartók's Fourth Quartet, with its pizzicato movement . . . The net-formations, which were very soft until this point, now become hard and mechanical: the movement is like a machine that breaks down . . . The fourth movement is a very brutal movement . . . very fast and threatening. Everything that had happened before is now crammed together . . . And the fifth movement – in great contrast with the compressed fourth – spreads itself out just, just . . . like a cloud.[2]

The shared 'concept' is partly a matter of rhyming movements, as in the Cello Concerto, but it perhaps also has to do with interpenetrations between total chromaticism and the pure intervals of the harmonic series, particularly the octave and the fifth,[3] which come easily to string instruments by virtue of their tuning and also their readiness to sound overtones. The rhyming and the harmonic-chromatic interference are both featured at the end of the first movement, where a descending chromatic scale is heard in the fluting sounds of harmonics in octaves, creating a magical reinterpretation of a basic musical image, as so often in Ligeti. Then 'the collapse at the end of the first movement returns as a variant at the end of the second movement. It is like a rhyme between two lines of a poem.'[4]

The music is altogether full of harmonics, exactingly notated, and it was largely this aspect that was responsible for the delayed première: the LaSalle Quartet, for whom it was written, needed more than a year in which to learn it. Example 5 (pages 66–7) shows a passage from the first movement where the cello is sounding progressively higher harmonics on its G string, the eighth partial eventually being reinforced, or collected, by the leader, in a context of rustling chromatic motion that characteristically jitters between wide intervals and scale-like patterns.

Technically demanding, the quartet also requires extreme agility
of mind. As Ligeti has said: 'The entire string quartet tradition from
Beethoven to Webern is there somewhere in the quartet, even
sonata form, although only like an immured corpse.'[5] This was the
springtime of postmodernist collage (Berio's *Sinfonia* dates from
the same period), but Ligeti evokes rather than quotes, and his
evocations are so fine as to be felt lying just over the horizon of
what is heard. Webern's Bagatelles op.9 are suggested by the
gauze-thin textures, the treble register, and indeed the abundance of
harmonics, while the shape of the movements and their constructed
expressionism brings the work closer to Berg's Lyric Suite, whose
markings are imitated (Allegro nervoso and Prestissimo sfrenato in
the first movement). Inevitably Bartók is there, and not only in the
third movement. And sometimes the music spreads its feelers
beyond the world of the string quartet: to *The Rite of Spring*, as
Ligeti has suggested of the fourth movement, or at the start of the
fifth to the undulating minor thirds of various Mahler openings.

Rather solider are the links that bind the quartet to its
companions within Ligeti's output: those minor thirds, for
example, rattle on from *Continuum*, and there are several moments
where the music appears to draw back in order to reveal, as if in the
distance, the 'Ligeti chord' of minor third plus major second. This
is heard twice in the first movement, as F–A♭–B♭ (bar 19) and as
that chord's tritone transposed inversion – its opposite, as it might
be – B–D–E (bar 70); it also crops up prominently in the fourth
movement and the finale. Moreover, the first movement's sequence
of cello harmonics reveals that one source for this chord could be
the piling-up of the sixth, seventh and eighth overtones (D–F–G in
this case), and it may be this rooting high in the harmonic series
that accounts for the harmony's hovering restedness.

As much as in *Lontano*, though, definable harmonies are the
intermittent products of musical processes which seem to gain their
energies from elsewhere – in this case principally from games of
imitation and from rhythmic schemes of ostinato or of progressive
acceleration or deceleration. Because speed is used as a supple

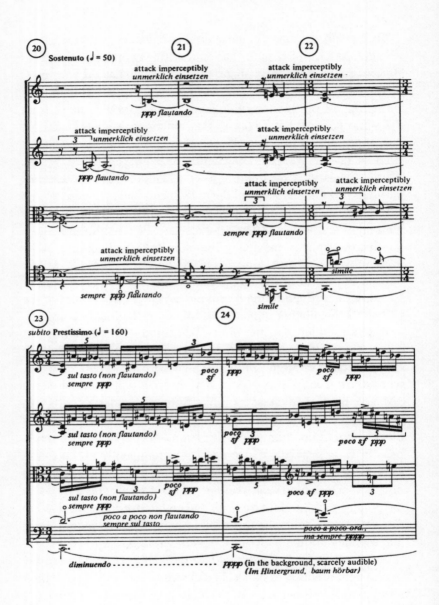

Example 5 From the first movement of the Second String Quartet

structural force, it is never stable: there are no slow movements in this quartet and no scherzos, but rather gravity and rush (also wit) remain possibilities for any movement at any time. The first movement is concerned very much with abrupt changes from slow to fast and back again, with vigorous gallops being suddenly braked into stillness, and then as suddenly set racing again. On the melodic level, these changes are equalled by transitions from highly angular motion to tremolando. The second movement introduces specified quarter-tones into the cluster image; the third is a further essay in machine music, marked 'como un meccanismo di precisione'. The fourth is a kind of compression of everything that has occurred hitherto, after which the finale seems to belong in a world of its own, a world which it opens and closes with its wobbling minor thirds. It is, Ligeti has said, 'a mild variant of the devilish first movement, as if from afar, like the "Lacrimosa" to the Requiem movements'.[6] The work, which had become very physical and near in its fourth movement, withdraws again from us.

As he was writing the quartet's finale, the composer was reminded of the spasmodic changes of locale in Lewis Carroll's *Alice* books, which he has described as 'probably as important to me as Kafka',[7] and which, more than twenty years later, were to become the subject of a projected opera. More immediately he remained through the looking glass in the work he went straight on to write in August–December 1968, which was again a chamber piece in several movements, but these much shorter: the Ten Pieces for wind quintet. Partly because of the change of medium, the images are sharper and brighter than in the quartet. There is little of the iridescent uncertainty that the quartet gains from living in a mountaintop world of harmonics; the music is direct, colourful, clear and compact: a bag of tricks.

The original plan proposed a succession of five 'micro-concertos', one for each instrument, contained between two ensemble pieces. However, since the concertos all turned out fast, Ligeti felt the need to separate them: hence the definitive series of Ten Pieces, with the even-numbered movements spotlighting the clarinet, flute, oboe, horn and bassoon, in that order. Somewhat disguising this scheme is the fact that the concertante element is pretty pervasive, with all the players featuring all through as soloists (which is also the case in the Cello Concerto). For example, the finale depends not only on the comic swagger of the bassoon but on the abruptness and curiosity of everyone else, and the horn draws out its melody into an atmosphere created by tremblings from flute, clarinet and bassoon in the manner of the Second Quartet's finale. (This passage was originally intended to function here too as conclusion, and was only at a later stage tacked on to the horn's movement.) There is also a general movement throughout the set from dark to light, the flautist and oboist moving up the scales of their instrumental families (from alto flute to standard flute to piccolo, from cor anglais to oboe d'amore to oboe).

In a chain of pieces so short, most of them only lasting a minute, utmost variety is a good formal principle. Yet there do seem to be deliberate cross-references: the heavily accented chords cutting up silence in the second and seventh movements, for instance, or the major seconds sprinkled across key moments, or the way the sixth movement emerges as an alternative to the fifth (they began as a single movement, and retain the same marking). Also, the work is given a larger shape by changes in its dramatis personae – not only in terms of rising registers but of striking absences. Most noticeably, the oboist is silent in the fourth and fifth movements, of which the fourth also excludes the horn. The entrance of the oboe in the sixth piece – for the first time, since it is at this point that the player switches from oboe d'amore – is splendidly dramatic, as if, as Ligeti has put it, 'an actor in peculiarly bright costume has been absent from the stage, and then unexpectedly came on and for a while played the leading part.' After this moment of glory, the instrument gets buried in the ensemble (in a shrieking ensemble with high clarinet and piccolo in the ninth movement, where the cloud style goes frantic in search of combination tones[8]) or else plays just a bit part, suggesting that Ligeti retained his doubts about the oboe's excessive presence.

Quite as astonishing as the sudden entrance of the oboe is the unprepared appearance of melody – of '"dragonfly"-melodies,'⁹ as Ligeti aptly calls them, that descend and dissolve at the end of the seventh movement. These magical tunes are still emerging from the simple chromatic scale that had served Ligeti on earlier occasions, as at the end of the Second Quartet's opening movement; their wings are yet wet. But they add a miraculous and prophetic touch to a work of great charm, elegance and wit. The last words in the score are left to Lewis Carroll:

. . . but–' There was a long pause.
'Is that all?' Alice timidly asked.
'That's all,' said Humpty Dumpty. 'Good-bye.'

By calling his string quartet of 1968 'no.2', Ligeti effectively acknowledged his *Métamorphoses nocturnes* of 1953–4 as no.1 and showed himself ready to look again at what he had achieved in Budapest. The pre-emigration quartet had been given a performance (its first) in Vienna in 1958, but since then Ligeti had not shown much interest in the works of his previous self. It was as if the annihilation of harmony, melody and rhythm in *Atmosphères* had been also an annihilation of the music he had composed hitherto. Now in the late sixties, though, he was beginning to rediscover chords and tunes, and to reapproach the standard genres; the advance was also a return journey to the past, including his own past. Early in 1969, when the Ten Pieces had recently been completed, a Budapest-period wind quintet, the Six Bagatelles, was played complete for the first time, and the next year, also in Sweden, came the first performance of two choral settings made in 1955 of poems by Sándor Weöres, 'Night' and 'Morning'. *Musica ricercata*, the set of piano pieces from which the quintet bagatelles were arranged, also had some limited dissemination, but for the moment these few works were all the world was allowed to see of Ligeti before the age of thirty-five. This was as much of a window as he was yet prepared to open.

It is a window into a very Bartókian world, for the simple reason that Bartók's music was, at this stage, the most advanced Ligeti knew. The First Quartet indicates this very clearly, though it already includes a number of more specifically Ligetian features, including the wish to find a freer sort of unfolding (here through a concatenation of episodes bound by reference to a motif which magically first emerges, in the form G–A–G♯–A♯, as a variation on parallel chromatic scales), and, on a more detailed level, the progressive expansion and contraction of intervals to move from oscillations to more jagged contours and back again (in the Prestissimo towards the close), as well as the first signs of a concern with string harmonics. The connection between the quartets – or, rather, the astonishing gulf, given that Ligeti was a fully mature musician when he wrote the First, and that the Second came only a decade and a half later – is mirrored also between the sets of movements for wind quintet, except that the scoring now suggests Stravinsky's Octet as antecedent rather than Bartók. Like the Ten Pieces, the Six Bagatelles display rhythmic verve, clean colour and perfect, surprising miniature form, but of course they are in every way simpler and more symmetrical.

In their original form, that of movements in *Musica ricercata*, these delightful pieces take on a more teasing character as elements in a progressive extension of resources. The first movement of the piano volume is played almost entirely on the As of the keyboard, to which D is added right at the end: otherwise, monotone and octave-spanning ideas are combined in what has to be largely a rhythmic machine. Similarly, the second movement is based mostly on two notes, E♯ and F♯, in hymn-like strains which are played against a third note, G, in the second half. Ligeti's choice of three notes is a C minor triad, with the major third as useful interloper; then four notes provide him with the material for a barrel-organ number, and so on. The playfulness is characteristic – though characteristic more of Ligeti as he entered old age. In particular, the finale, where the presence at last of all the notes allows for a twelve-note theme heard in counterpoint with

descending chromatic scales, looks right forward to the more
intricate canons of the Etudes.

The two choral pieces, composed the year before Ligeti's
emigration, are closer to the music of his first decade in the west –
especially the first of them, which starts out as an eight-part canon
building up white-note clusters in crescendo and then switches to a
black-note chord. This use of elementary procedures with a
startling precision and unusualness parallels the poetic technique of
Weöres, whom Ligeti has described as 'my favourite poet'.[10] For
example, the cluster canon in 'Night' repeats just two words,
'rengeteg tövis', which carry suggestions of an impenetrable,
thorny, fairytale forest, and the black-note chord sounds out at
'csönd' (silence).[11]

7

Ramifications

The extraordinary group of works Ligeti produced in 1967–8 – *Lontano*, *Continuum*, the Second Quartet and the Ten Pieces for wind quintet – had greatly enlarged the scope of his music, principally by reintroducing the resource of harmony. Some of the possibilities can be seen at their simplest in the Ten Pieces, of which the first, for instance, begins with an initial white-note chord (E–F–G–A–B) that is gradually clouded with chromatic displacements, so that it vanishes and re-emerges like an object seen in swirling mist, throughout which the single note C♯ is reserved until it suddenly takes over all by itself, luminously scored for alto flute and cor anglais in unison, a bright fortissimo ray in total contrast with what has gone before. These two modes of change, the almost imperceptible and the abrupt, had been basic features of Ligeti's music since *Atmosphères*. Now, with harmony, their range was vastly greater.

The next work to exploit that range was *Ramifications* (winter 1968–9), in which Ligeti returned to the sonority of strings, but to a twelve-part group, whether of soloists or multiples. Half the ensemble (three violins, viola, cello and bass) is tuned normally; the other half (four violins, viola and cello) plays a quarter-tone sharp, so that the composer has at his disposal a fine grid of quarter-tones without any player having to produce intervals smaller than a semitone. Clusters can thus be denser, as at the opening, where fluctuations in the style of *Continuum* bring in every middle-register note between G half-sharp and B♭, with the striking exception of the A that is the very foundation of the tuning.

Also, quite straightforward harmonies, like the major third (bars 11–12) can be rendered strange and indefinite when they arrive at once in two different intonations.

These are the uses of quarter-tones, to thicken and estrange, with which Ligeti is concerned in *Ramifications*: to similar ends he had asked for microtonal deviations in parts of the Second Quartet – in addition to those deviations that will likely arise when so much of the music exists in the twilight world of harmonics. *Ramifications* has very much less to do with harmonics (though they make an eerie entrance towards the end of the piece), but the interferences of the orchestras, sitting close together, produce a comparable distortion. Exact quarter-tone separation is not crucial; in any event, the two ensembles will tend to draw together (perhaps particularly if the larger scoring is used) in ways that the composer cannot and does not wish to foresee. As in *Harmonies*, he relishes the smudge. 'Only in a few structurally dense places are there approximate quarter-tone clusters; elsewhere, and especially in passages where the musical texture is transparent and closely stitched, there is a new sort of "uncertain" harmony, which produces an effect of "spoiling" the harmonic formations of equal temperament, and sometimes of diatonicism. The harmonies smell high: decomposition is drawn into the music.'[1]

It is, though, a sweet rot. The basic procedure is that of *Continuum* and *Coulée*, whereby harmonic fields are established, extended, superimposed and dissolved as textures of repeating patterns, and there are two broad phases of change. The first opens out from the starting cluster to the sullied major third, to a fourth, and then, by means of quasi-diatonic arpeggios, a fifth. There is a closing-in at the treble end, and all the lines draw up to a high E (in two different tunings, of course), long sustained and joined by harmonics. The second part starts with a shift to gruff melodic tritones in the bass, these going on into a long line that slips chromatically like something out of a late Romantic symphony, while swarming repetitive figures return above, and grow this time from a hyperchromatic cluster into an echoing of intervals tossed from one group to the other. Again the maximum expansion is reached in wide arpeggiations, out of which there suddenly come forceful, muscular melodies that fall to leave a low F in the double bass, the ensemble's bottom-most note. This is denatured by the player's addition of harmonics, one of which, a thin stratospheric C, is taken up by a violin (a gesture analogous to that in the last bar of Example 5), and then other harmonics enter in other instruments. Soft asynchronous jitters begin throughout the ensemble, but just as everyone has agreed on the same equal quivering, the music is torn off in a typical Ligeti ending.

The next page on the calendar was the Chamber Concerto for thirteen players (1969–70), which follows further ramifications of Ligetian principles, corresponds in its multi-movement form with the Second Quartet (as 'light sister' to that work, in the composer's phrase), and again sports in the instrumental playground of the Ten Pieces. According to Ligeti, *Ramifications* had been 'an endpoint in the development from "dense and static" to "broken-up and moving"' textures – a development that had been realized in different ways in *Lontano* and *Continuum*. The very title had referred to 'the polyphonic technique of part-writing: first bound together in a knot, the individual parts move divergently, so that the bundle of voices gradually disperses, and so the music seems actually to ramify'.[2] But *Ramifications* turned out not to be a finale after all. If there is indeed a culmination to Ligeti's early years in the west – a work that marks off those years as a distinct period of response to a time of rapid technological progress and intellectual excitement – then it came in the Chamber Concerto.

The work was written for the Viennese modern-music ensemble Die Reihe, led by Friedrich Cerha, who, as a composer, had found himself in a similar situation to Ligeti's in the late fifties and early sixties. (Ligeti, fully aware of the proximity, had written a programme note on his *Relazioni fragili*, a piece played by Die Reihe in 1960.) The title 'Chamber Concerto' is meant to indicate that all the players are soloists, but perhaps its more important

virtue is its neutrality, which is a quality Ligeti has consistently
sought in naming works whose multiplicities of movements, and
therefore of characters, would have made a poetic title
inappropriate: hence his five concertos and flatly titled chamber
works. (The only exception is the set of three pieces for two pianos,
where the problem is solved by an evocative title in three parts for
the three movements: *Monument – Selbstportrait – Bewegung*.)

Example 6 Plan of the opening of the Chamber Concerto

Of the Chamber Concerto's four movements, the first, Corrente,
begins once more fixed in the bottom half of the treble staff, like
Lontano, the second movement of the Second Quartet, and
Ramifications. The sound, though, is new: lazy and ambling, as
flute and clarinet wander in loose canon among the five chromatic
notes from G♭ to B♭, supported by slower movements within the
same pitch space from the bass clarinet (which replaces the bassoon, and so helps give the piece a more vibrant sound) and the low
strings in harmonics. Structurally this movement is one of the
simplest in Ligeti so far – to the extent that its harmonic essentials
can be represented in a compact abstract: Example 6. The opening
cluster gradually widens to span a fifth, and then narrows at the top
end into a C♯–D trill in the strings; all the way, of course, the micropolyphonic weave works through changing colours and densities.
Until now, through thirty-seven bars, the music has been cramped
into a box of nine notes, so the effect is hugely liberating, like the
arrival of C♯ in the first of the Ten Pieces, when the whole pitch
space is all at once opened up by E♭s across five octaves. In one

sense E♭ is the expected next note, since the music has been inching upwards by chromatic degrees, but of course the sonority of octaves and the wide range are entirely new, and the gesture exemplifies very simply how Ligeti can follow a strict plan in a surprising way. The E♭ is then characteristically confused by the addition of other pitches, from Hammond organ and brass, and there emerge new clusters outside the domain of the original one. At this point, too, comes a broad but brief melodic statement from all the wind instruments in octaves, using the notes of the bottom cluster (D–G), but starting almost like a massively amplified folktune (D–E–G–F . . .) The final surprise comes in the last few bars, when the music explodes out of its cluster constraints so that the instruments, as soloists and in groups, can begin to find much more various and particular kinds of melody. Then the clamp comes down once more, and just two notes are left. The whole plan is utterly simple, but in the execution, with fluid textures, bright colours and incipient melodies, is made astonishing. Perhaps, once again, harmony is to be considered not as the music's motive force but rather as a beautiful illusion: 'My general idea for [the first] movement,' Ligeti has remarked, 'was the surface of a stretch of water, where everything takes place below the surface.'[3]

The following movement has a typical Ligeti marking for movements of slow, quiet change ('Calmo, sostenuto'), though the music is quite unlike anything he had written before. It starts with an eight-note chord which is almost a pile of triads; this then turns in instrumentation and harmony, and is absorbed into the Hammond organ, out of which it gives rise to very soft jostling movements in other instruments. These become the background for melodic figures from a plaintive trio of horn, oboe d'amore and trombone – figures in which fifths and triads are again often paramount, enhancing the Romantic echo, though the harmonic colours change as much as the instrumental ones, until everything comes to congeal into a whole-tone chord from the central trio (C–D–E), and from that into a cluster (D–E♭–E), brayed fortissimo. After that – rather as with the entrance of octaves in the first movement (and as in the Second Quartet, the movements can be regarded as substitute versions of the same principle) – comes an abrupt change to neighbouring simplicity, as if something absolutely inevitable and yet totally unexpected had turned up around the corner: as the cluster dies away, the tritone B–F is heard sounding quietly in octaves, recalling a tritone moment in *Lontano*. From this develops a second part of the movement, surmounted by insistent flurries from high woodwinds and violins, and abating towards a new eight-note chord, whose upper part is a tower of fifths, and which disintegrates to leave a solitary G in octaves.

The third movement has to some degree the formal profile of the first, and so reinforces the distorting-mirror relationships among the movements. It begins within a narrow middle-register compass, and reaches its first marked disjunction with a new note in octaves (A♭ in the twelfth bar). It also ends just as something new has been glimpsed. However, the heading is 'Movimento preciso e mec-canico', and, quite unlike the quietly flowing first movement, this is the most fantastical of Ligeti's clockworks, a disconnected chirruping of regular rhythms from different odd ensembles that might suggest one of Heath Robinson's contraptions or the 'twittering machines' of Paul Klee. There is some authority for this latter reference, for Klee and Miró are the painters to whom Ligeti would most often refer at this time, and for obvious reasons. Both were inventors of clearly constructed worlds, whose rules and elements they precisely defined. Both loved colour and playfulness and strangeness and simplicity. Life's comedy, in both, exists on the brink. So it is in Ligeti, and his enjoyment of the octave (a curiously rare sound in western music) is like Miró's enjoyment of primary colour.

The presto finale of the Chamber Concerto continues the mechanical feeling a little, but the twitterings are now rustlings that develop and echo in the manner of *Ramifications*, moving through clusters, single intervals and arpeggios, and racing around the small orchestra in a perpetuum mobile of great virtuosity. Once again, as in the first and second movements, one way out of the maze appears to be through melody, and a line starts out on the horn, most positive of instruments. It is a twelve-note theme, emphasizing the intervals that have been prominent throughout the movement: the major second (or minor seventh), the minor third and the tritone. However, in terms both of interval and instrumentation the melody quickly begins to lose its distinctiveness, and the perpetual motion continues until the tritone A–E♭, like a single light of gathering intensity, begins to shine through the texture and freeze the music, leaving only disjointed echoes.

8

Melodies

Even so, Ligeti had discovered – perhaps during the very process of composing – the usefulness of melody, and just as the last movement of the Requiem five years earlier had sighted the new worlds of *Lux aeterna* and *Lontano*, so the tentative melodic uncoiling of the Chamber Concerto's finale was a trial of what would turn out to be a new direction. The follow-up came very quickly, in a work which (provocatively for the time) makes its new musical interest quite apparent in its title: *Melodien* for orchestra (1971). This Ligeti wrote in Berlin, where he had gone on a one-year scholarship from the German Academic Exchange Service in 1969 and stayed until 1973; it was one of several pieces commissioned by the city of Nuremberg to celebrate the quincentenary of the birth of Albrecht Dürer.

By contrast with *Atmosphères* and *Lontano*, *Melodien* is devised for a chamber orchestra, and if the string parts are taken by soloists, as they may be, the ensemble is not much bigger than that of the Chamber Concerto (sixteen players, as against thirteen in the earlier work). Nevertheless, the feel of the piece is much more orchestral, as at the start, where a shimmering pattern of asynchronous chromatic scales ripples upwards in woodwinds, piano and strings, while trumpet and trombone softly embark on the first melodic essays and the double bass holds a harmonic G. The entire bright texture is placed in the treble, which is where the piece will have most of its existence, and these opening three bars are typical too in having three levels – sustained notes or chords, repeating figures out of *Continuum*, and the new melodies celebrated by the title – each to be observed through the other two.

As one might expect in a Ligeti composition, these three levels are not held distinct, but are forever dissolving into one another. A melody may stand still, on a note which becomes part of a

chord, or it may deteriorate into a rotating figure, and the other
fundamental elements are similarly intertransformable. At certain
points in the score, however, the separation is unusually clear:
one such moment is the first appearance of long melodic lines
(bars 25ff), from a group of violins and then from the violas,
while there are repetitive patterns in the piccolo, xylophone,
celesta and first violin, and long notes in other instruments (the
high A that lasts throughout is a cello harmonic). Example 7 is a
simplified version of the score to show these different layers.

Example 7 From Melodien *(simplified score)*

Perhaps the first point to note here is the intricacy and delicate beauty of Ligeti's melodies. Their qualities had been foreshadowed to some extent in the Chamber Concerto and the Ten Pieces, and even in the chromatic scale melodies of *Aventures* and the Second Quartet, but there had been little preparation for the density of loveliness and charm that applies through *Melodien*. It is as if the long suppression of melody in Ligeti's music had created a tension that is suddenly released in this work, rather as harmony had all at once flowered in *Lontano*. In his progressive rediscovery of the rudiments of music, melody brings with it not only a babbling surface delightfulness but also a new speed and variety of harmonic movement, and of this too there is some indication in the example above. As so often in Ligeti's harmony, the top is more stable than the bottom: the music reaches towards the treble rather than being rooted in the bass, and here the one constant feature is the high A, which dominates the whole first seventy bars, or almost half the piece. Nearly as consistently present, and reinforced by the melodies, is the D♭ or C♯ a minor sixth below (this interval of a minor sixth has great importance in *Melodien*, right from the start). Further down, the harmony is more fluid, and differently fluid in the three departments of the texture. As this passage proceeds, the chords tend to thin towards the top, while the melodies and repeating patterns drift downwards, the latter taking the initiative – pulling the melodies down, as it were, while these melodies sound at their successive highpoints the notes that are to be retained as important in a sequence of fourths: D♭–A♭/G♯–E♭/D♯. Nor can it be fortuitous that the viola melody begins by picking out a near inversion of the violin melody, or that later the two lines mimic each other. Such mirrorings and shadowings – which had been compounded and thereby obscured in the micropolyphonies of such works as the Requiem – are now revealed in finer textures, forking through the music and contributing much to its mazy bewilderment.

The passage in Example 7 arrives at a point where the piece is moving towards more complex harmonic fields – though not as complex as those it will explore in its second half. At other moments the harmonic movement is much more unidirectional and simple. For instance, near the start, once the rising scales have come to rest on their highpoint – the same high A observed in the example – harmony begins to breed out of unison. The F a major third below is added, and then the E♭ below that, creating a whole-tone moment, and then other notes in quicker succession as the harmony moves towards the richness it will need to support the first melodic unfoldings from violins and violas. After this sequence, the drift of chords, ostinatos and melodies continues until the two horns come forward in a developed re-enactment of the Brucknerian moment from the end of *Lontano* (bars 60ff). This presages a rapid simplification to octave Cs, out of which another cycle of proliferation begins, to lead eventually to more rising chromatic scales in a passage of fluorescent brilliance (bars 110ff). The scales disintegrate; there is another horn duet (bars 136ff); and the music disappears into extremes of pitch, with high harmonics in the violins and a low E in the double bass part.

With that ending – a typical departure into imaginable other regions – melodic exuberance went out of Ligeti's music for the moment. In his next piece, the Double Concerto for flute, oboe and orchestra (1972), there is little melody until towards the end: this coda re-enacts the last-minute liberation of the Chamber Concerto's first movement, and in other respects, too, the work follows closely on its predecessors. Like the Ten Pieces, the Chamber Concerto and *Melodien* (or indeed the rescued Bagatelles), it shows Ligeti's joy in the pure colours of woodwinds – not only in its solo parts but also in its orchestration, for an ensemble of full symphonic woodwind, modest brass, three players on tuned percussion instruments and just fourteen strings, with no violins. Again like the three works that came immediately before, it has points where attention is focused on the oboe d'amore, which is almost a personal signature in Ligeti's scores of this period. (It will turn up again in

Clocks and Clouds, San Francisco Polyphony and *Le Grand Macabre*.) Nevertheless, the Double Concerto is unusual in the subdued character it maintains almost throughout its first movement, and never quite shakes off in its second.

As a two-movement form it has affinities with the Cello Concerto and *Apparitions*, especially since the movements are slow (Calmo, con tenerezza) then fast (Allegro corrente). The slow movement is one of effortful harmonic change, more laboured than in the comparable second movements of the Second Quartet and the Chamber Concerto. Starting out from a whole-tone chord in the composer's favoured middle register, the music draws and discloses further chordal veils, sometimes revealing the light of a simple harmony: the tritone B–F again, the fifth A–E, and then, at the principal climax, a unison B♭ in the strings which grows in intensity before the music fans out with increasing confidence to octave G♯s and beyond, is pricked and flops into subaqueous regions where the main voice is that of the bass flute. These are the main stations. The phases in between are more clouded and disconcerting from Ligeti's use of quarter-tones, which, as in *Ramifications*, thicken chromatic clusters and set up a rival tuning system.

Microtones had moved into the background in the Chamber Concerto and *Melodien* – though they are there in that background, for, as Ligeti has pointed out in connection with the Chamber Concerto, 'you automatically get a micro-intervallic deviation, since you can never find a piano, a celesta and an organ all tuned exactly to the same temperament'.[1] The return of small intervals in the Double Concerto may have been prompted by one of the discoveries he made during the time he spent in 1972 at Stanford University, California – that of the music and instruments of Harry Partch – for he has referred to the 'Partch effects' in this work. Just as Partch's music sounds odd and even wonky to ears used to equal temperament, so the Double Concerto – like *Ramifications*, though with the benefit of Ligeti's rapid development since – sets up within itself off-tunings: 'That is what interested me, the effect of music where the tuning systems clash; it is like a body in a state of gradual decomposition . . . My feeling is that both diatonic and chromatic music have been worn out. I do not think we need to look for other tonal systems – I abhor all fixed systems; what I really want is the effect of deviation from either pure or equal temperament.[2]

The first movement is begun by the orchestral flutes and generally led by the solo flautist, playing alto flute until the final deflation. The solo oboist is a less frequent visitor, and the oboe's bright high register is used only at the bright tritone moment and the climax. This instrument comes into its own, though, in the second movement, which has much more the equality of a double concerto (none the less, the soloists are heard in alternation much more than in dialogue), and which is largely occupied with quick fluctuating oscillations in the manner of the Chamber Concerto's finale, except in one passage of even and exact note repetitions in the machine style of that work's third movement. Another connection is with the eighth of the Ten Pieces, at least at the start, where the music is similarly a flux of minor third D–F vibrations, and similarly scored, though moved down an octave to where it can be played by bass flute, bass clarinet and clarinets in their bottom register. Further cross-references come near the end of the work, where an eruptive upward glissando signals the final evaporation, as in the last movement of the Chamber Concerto and *Melodien*. However, the second movement of the Double Concerto is unlike any of these models in its unstable twinning of deviant tunings, and in a specially attractive and versatile feature: the use of solo instruments – not necessarily the principal soloists – to throw melodic cascades from one harmonic field to another, one spangled screen of tremulations to the next. As Ligeti has remarked: 'The music glitters as though deep-frozen and moves as stiffly as a puppet.'

9

Clocks and Clouds and Polyphonies

In 1973, the year after the Double Concerto, Ligeti took up an appointment as professor of composition at the music academy in Hamburg, which since then has been his main home. As in Budapest in the fifties, or Stockholm in the sixties, teaching provided not only financial security but a sounding board: the stimulus of younger colleagues, and of opportunities to develop ideas. But there was also another aspect to his professional life, an aspect which so far this survey has ignored, for all through the time from *Lux aeterna* to the Double Concerto he had also in mind a project for an opera.

The commission had come from the Royal Opera of Stockholm, soon after the première in that city of the Requiem in 1965. *Aventures* and *Nouvelles aventures* were then still quite new, and Ligeti's first plan was for an evening-long entertainment in the same style: 'It will not be an opera in the usual sense. I cannot, will not, compose a traditional "opera"; for me the genre is irrelevant today, belonging as it does to a historical phase totally different from the present compositional situation.'[1] His idea was instead to write a piece for the resources of an opera house, under the title *Kylwiria*, the name he had given to an imaginary world of his childhood. But he changed tack, partly because he decided that a full-length work would need a plot after all, and partly because Kagel's *Staatstheater*, produced in Hamburg in 1971, supplied the need for a work engaging the personnel of an opera company in anti-conventional pursuits. He turned to the Oedipus story, and began to develop ideas in collaboration with the Swedish director Göran Gentele, who, as director of the Stockholm opera, had been responsible for the commission. A comic-strip *Oedipus* was planned; by 1971 the libretto had been written, and there were musical sketches. Gentele, who had taken over the administration of the Metropolitan Opera, New York, was planning to return to Stockholm to stage the new opera in 1974.

In the summer of 1972, however, he died in a car crash on Sardinia. Ligeti felt unable to continue a project that had belonged to the two of them, and used the sketches in his next two works: *Clocks and Clouds* for orchestra with women's voices (1972–3), and *San Francisco Polyphony* for large orchestra (1973–4). It was, of course, a personal setback, but the wider world too was changing, as the hopefulness of the late sixties lapsed in the face of the stale realities of Nixon and Brezhnev, and as, within the narrower confines of contemporary music, idealism and community spirit gave way to factiousness. For Ligeti, the brilliant, highly inventive and exuberant, forward-looking period of the Second Quartet, Ten Pieces, Chamber Concerto and *Melodien* was over, and the Double Concerto had already marked a move into comparative sombreness.

Clocks and Clouds seems to reflect a period of uncertainty, which is perhaps one reason why it has remained one of Ligeti's least frequently performed works. It confirms previous achievements: the microtonal wavering of the Double Concerto, the luminescent orchestration of that work and of *Melodien* (with an ensemble even more decisively balanced in favour of woodwinds and tuned percussion), the circling of musical nebulae around firm harmonic pillars that are now and then disclosed. 'On the formal level,' Ligeti has said,

> *Clocks and Clouds* approaches *Atmosphères* and *Lontano*: a form that's flowing, static, but almost without clusters, and even almost without chromaticism. I really use harmonies in this piece (not tonal harmonies, but harmonies of much greater complexity). I often use the major third, the minor third and the neutral third (which is between the two), and

the different degrees of transformation between the major
second and the minor third, as well as between the major
third and the perfect fourth.[2]

One new feature is the presence of voices, for the first time
since *Lux aeterna*, singing syllables chosen for sonority, not
meaning, the chorus being effectively a department of the
orchestra. The title, from an essay by Karl Popper, draws
attention to a distinction between phenomena of measurable
properties and others that can be defined only in general terms,
and its use here is the first evidence that Ligeti was seeing his
work within a larger intellectual context: much more evidence of
that was to come in the eighties and nineties. The clocks and
clouds had always been there in his music, certainly from as far
back as *Musica ricercata*; here they have their classic form in
Continuum-like regular patterns and drifting textures, which
interpenetrate throughout the course of the piece.

One thing Ligeti neglected in *Clocks and Clouds*, as he had in
the Double Concerto, was the busy proliferation of melodies that
had been let loose by *Melodien*. But that was an omission he
corrected in *San Francisco Polyphony*, which owes its title less
to philosophy than to geography, and to the circumstance of
having been commissioned by the San Francisco Symphony
Orchestra, for whom he created his first work for full symphony
orchestra since *Lontano* – and so far his last, since his subsequent
concertos are, like the earlier ones, for smaller formations. That
such a master of the orchestra should have produced only four big
concert pieces – *Apparitions*, *Atmosphères*, *Lontano* and *San
Francisco Polyphony* – perhaps says as much about the problems
of rehearsing new orchestral music in the late twentieth century
as it does about his own wishes and inclinations.

To quote his note on *San Francisco Polyphony*:

There is an interplay of order and chaos: the individual
melodic lines are regular; their combination, either

simultaneously or successively, is chaotic; in the overall form, however, in the overruling progress of musical events, order is again to be found. One might imagine individual objects which are hurled in the greatest disarray into a drawer, and yet the drawer itself has a clearly defined form.[3]

As to what that form is, again his own words provide the best outline:

The way I see its structure is this: the exposition of the musical material creates a chromatic space that is filled up with heterogeneous tunes which are different from, and stand in contrast to, one another. The space then gets less dense, as if someone went through it with a comb, thinning it out; the introduction ends on a high note (the introduction to *Melodien* is much the same), then follows the middle section, the longest part of the work, where twisting ostinatos whirl around long, expressive melodies. Gradually the musical texture gets polarized between the higher and the lower registers; at the two poles density increases, leaving an expanding empty space in the middle. Ultimately the melodic texture is squashed to the ceiling and the floor, and it all ends in a C across several octaves; every tune has been eliminated, as if ironed out, reduced to one note. At this point the coda begins, a kind of perpetuum mobile machine-like music.[4]

Half-jokingly, he has further suggested that the music, with its shapes that come and go in bewildering textures of melodies and ostinatos, responds to the fog of the city for which it was written.

While I was working on *San Francisco Polyphony* I thought that the city's atmosphere had a decisive influence on the music, but when I heard it performed I realized it is more Viennese: there are a number of expressive melodies in it reminiscent of Alban Berg or Mahler. Only the end of the piece, the prestissimo section, with its machine-like, hectic quality makes you think of a big American city.[5]

This was, indeed, his only American commission, though the fact is reflected perhaps less in the perpetuum mobile, for which there are parallels in the Chamber Concerto and the Double Concerto, than in the emphatic final gesture – something unusual in his music. As for the resemblance to Berg or Mahler, any such connection is undercut by his characteristic objectivity. The melodies, however expressive, never carry the music's whole-hearted voice: there are too many of them at a time, usually, and always they exist in a larger context of sustained tones and repeating patterns. It is as with the harmonies of *Lontano*, that they are froth – but highly appealing froth – on the surface of something else. One might even say that Ligeti's 'reintroduction' of melody was, as yet, rather a display of its continued exclusion.

Clocks and Clouds and *San Francisco Polyphony* belong not only to the aftermath of *Oedipus* but to the foremath of *Le Grand Macabre*, since they were completed between his decision to embark on this project and the start of the opera's composition. Once he had got going, he was to devote himself to the goal of the Stockholm première until it took place, in 1978, with only one brief interlude in the spring of 1976 for the three pieces for two pianos, *Monument – Selbstportrait – Bewegung*, written for the brothers Aloys and Alfons Kontarsky.

The Kontarskys then held a special place as exponents of two-piano music: it was for them that Stockhausen had written *Mantra* (1970), and inevitably their repertory also included the Boulez work Ligeti had in part analysed in the fifties: *Structures*. He might have been reminded of that fact, for the first piece in his cycle, *Monument*, is as elaborately and ostentatiously constructed as the first of Boulez's, even reaching to a similar maximum of six quite separate layers. It is not, of course, a serial composition, but it has little of the cheerful assortment of *San Francisco Polyphony*. Yet one has to take into account the matter of genre, for all Ligeti's works since *Continuum* and *Coulée* had been for orchestral resources, and *Monument* is in some sense a return to the more mechanistic world of those earlier keyboard pieces, and indeed of *Musica ricercata*.

The machine of *Monument* is one of expanding-contracting rhythmic patterns working on reiterations of fixed pitches in octaves: an initial A is repeated every 16-17-18-17-16-15-14-15-16 semiquavers, and so on; the next note, G♭, repeats at intervals of 8-9-10-9-8-7-6-7-8 semiquavers, and so on. Each new note thus brings with it a different pulsation, and each pulsation is slightly irregular, as if made by an ill-running metronome. When six different notes, and six different rhythmic cycles, have been introduced, the system begins to go haywire, and turns into regular semiquavers that lift off to the very top of the keyboard in both pianos.[6]

The second movement, *Selbsportrait*, is in full a 'Self-portrait with Reich and Riley (and Chopin is also there)', paying homage to the American practitioners of repetitive music whose work Ligeti had discovered when he was in California in 1972, but doing so within a style that grows recognizably out of *Continuum*. (Yet another of the composer's Californian discoveries, made in San Francisco at that time, was the work of M.C. Escher, whose metamorphic patterns and contradictory perspectives may be recalled by all three of these two-piano pieces.[7]) Almost throughout the self-portrait, some or other keys are being silently depressed, and this not only adds a pearly aura of sympathetic resonances to the quick scales and arpeggios of which the movement is largely composed, it also converts even rhythms into uneven ones, since beats are missed when one hand runs over the keys held by the other: Ligeti's performance instructions acknowledge that the idea came from Karl-Grik Welin, who used this technique in *Volumina*, and that it was further developed by Henning Siedentopf.[8] Ligeti has also remarked on

> ... a touch of irony (and no less self-irony, as I also depicted
> myself), combining Riley's pattern repetition and Reich's
> phase shifting with my own techniques of superimposed
> grids and supersaturated canons. Thus originated the triple
> portrait Riley-Reich-Ligeti, and in the background, like a
> phantom, the figure of Chopin can also be glimpsed:
> towards the end of the piece the different rhythmic layers
> are brought together, as a telescope is closed, in a joint
> presto unisono. The presto from Chopin's B♭ minor sonata
> is not actually quoted, but there is a faint allusion to the
> character of its movement, and the aura of the eminently
> pianistic is evoked.

Contrary to the first piece, this one ends by sinking into the far
bass.

That sort of rhyme, to use Ligeti's term again, is a hint that the
three pieces are rearrangements of each other, and indeed the last
of them, *Bewegung* ('Motion'), can be heard as a molten version
of the first, with the stark octave chords turned into arpeggios that
tumble with lustrous brilliance: the full title of the piece is 'With
tender flowing motion'. What links the two movements is partly
the canonic principle, for almost concealed behind the flickering
surface of *Bewegung* is a canon in eight voices. Only at the end
do the arpeggios clear to leave a mirror canon that is also a
chorale in wooden, puppet chords: a solution that is also a puzzle
of its own.

10

Le Grand Macabre

According to Ligeti's own account, the idea of basing his Stockholm opera on the play *La Balade du Grand Macabre*, by the Belgian writer Michel de Ghelderode, came at the end of 1972 from Aliute Meczies, eventually the designer of the first production; Gentele, and the *Oedipus* project, had been dead only a few months. Ligeti remembered having heard the author's name once before: 'Some years previously, in the smoky Darmstadt Schlosskeller, the Belgian composer Jacques Calonne . . . mentioned that Ghelderode would be something for me, but then his voice evaporated in the wine and the sounds of *Sergeant Pepper*.'[1] Now, under the rather different circumstances of the seventies, the usefulness of Ghelderode was clearer, and Michael Meschke, director of the Stockholm puppet theatre (and in due course of the opera's première), was given the task of condensing a flowery play into a form suitable for setting – the task of, in Ligeti's own term, 'Jarryfying' the drama. Meschke completed a first version at the end of March 1973, but Ligeti wanted the text concentrated further, and so a second version was prepared by the summer, a version that now satisfied the composer's need for something 'very intensive, tight and direct'. However, the libretto was altered further by Ligeti himself during the process of composition, which began in earnest in December 1974, following some sketching the previous summer.[2] *Clocks and Clouds* and *San Francisco Polyphony* were completed during this incubation period, and the opera follows the former work (as also the Double Concerto) in balancing its orchestra in favour of wind and tuned percussion.

The plot is simple but capacious, touching on human games as various as sex, politics and drinking. The overriding theme is death, which had been the theme too of the only other large-scale vocal work Ligeti had composed in the west: the Requiem. And because the Requiem was also his only other western work with solo singers enunciating meaningful language, some points of similarity were inevitable in terms of compositional technique – though the intervening decade has been a long one in Ligeti's life, and its fruits are displayed proudly on the pages of the opera.

The scene is laid in the imaginary kingdom of Breughelland, the country of peasants, monsters and apocalypses depicted in the works of the Breughels. This idea comes from Ghelderode, though it is certainly one that would have appealed to Ligeti, who has described the elder Breughel as one of his favourite painters, along with Bosch (not to mention Klee and Miró, and Altdorfer . . .). As for the music:

> The general stylistic features make up some kind of flea market. There is everything there: a traditional closing passacaglia, symphonic intermezzi, overture, fanfare, but everything is strangely transformed. It is half real, half unreal, a disintegrating, disorderly world where everything is falling in, breaking up. The overture is based on the opening fanfares of Monteverdi's *Orfeo* . . . [but] I have twelve old-fashioned car klaxons, [which] are brass instruments gone all wrong, symbolizing the general atmosphere of dilapidation and ruin. There are tonal passages, atonal ones, many quotations from music of past ages. All these go into my flea market.[3]

Following the motorhorn overture, which is a short palindrome, enter Piet the Pot, a high tenor, the opera's common man. He is drunk throughout the action. Before long he has been joined by a pair of young lovers, 'very beautiful in a Botticellian way' (both are played by women), originally called Spermando and Clitoria, then sagely changed to Amando and Miranda, of whom the latter was renamed again as Amanda, at a time when

Ligeti thought his music would be meeting another Miranda in a setting of *The Tempest*. If Ligeti had not had much experience in writing for voices, *Aventures* and *Nouvelles aventures* provided all the experience he needed in order to come up with kinds of vocal behaviour that would particularize different people and different situations to the point of caricature. Amando and Amanda, for instance, are almost always vocally as well as physically entwined in each other, and their Monteverdian embellishments (shown in Example 8) come near a pre-orgasmic panting. As so often in Ligeti, the music is ironic and serious at the same time: the joke, of a couple about to couple (and therefore of two characters who have no separate identities), is also a show of glamour and sensuality.

Example 8 From the first scene of Le Grand Macabre

This first Amando-Amanda duet, ending as above, is interrupted by another voice, which comes from a tomb. One calling himself 'Nekrotzar' emerges, and in his imperious baritone takes command of Piet, declaring that he has come to announce the end of the world: he is the 'Grand Macabre' of the title. He sends Piet off back to the tomb to fetch his paraphernalia – coat, hat, scythe, trumpet – and then mounts the poor man to ride off carrying his message of death and destruction. Amando and Amanda meanwhile have taken advantage of the empty tomb.

The second scene, again introduced by a motorhorn prelude, is concerned largely with a couple whose sexual needs are more waning and exotic: the astrologer Astradamors (bass) and his wife Mescalina (mezzo), he wearing women's underwear over his trousers, she clad entirely in leather and brandishing a whip. Once their activities have come to a satisfactory conclusion, she dispatches him to his telescope, through which he observes, muttering mumbo jumbo, while she has an erotic vision of the goddess Venus. Nekrotzar then enters on Piet's back, and turns his attention on Mescalina, who is coming out of her Venusian dream, having loudly demanded a man who is well hung. Nekrotzar declares himself to fit the bill, and in a violent embrace he kills her, first victim of the 'dies irae'. The first act ends climactically in a demonic, exultant trio for the three men, who set off together for the palace.

This is the setting for the third scene, which has another mechanical prelude, this time for electric bells. The palace is that of the ruler of Breughelland, the boy prince Go-Go (the part is taken by a boy treble or high counter-tenor), who is besieged by two warring politicians, the White Minister and the Black. Driven beyond endurance by the bickering between this smug pair, the prince astonishes them by accepting their resignations, but before the argument can go forward, the stage is invaded by the Chief of the Secret Police and agents. The Police Chief is sung by a coloratura soprano, who appears in three disguises (as bird of prey, spider and octopus) and each time delivers a message of warning in nonsense code made the more undecipherable by musical acrobatics. (Her party pieces are separately available as *Mysteries of the Macabre*, which also exists in a version for coloratura trumpeter.) Eventually – after Go-Go has mimed a speech to popular acclamation in a parody of the theatricals of dictatorship – the threat is revealed to be that of Nekrotzar, who makes his entry during a big orchestral set piece, entitled 'Collage'.

As Ligeti describes it:

I composed a kind of synthetic folk music whose actual constituent elements are genuine folk tunes. Nekrotzar is accompanied by four musicians, four masked devils. One is a violinist who plays a Scott Joplin-type ragtime on his violin, which is deliberately mistuned. The bassoon player intones a distorted Greek Orthodox hymn. That is the tune we used to sing at Easter at the Romanian secondary school where I was a pupil . . . The third devil plays a mixture of a Brazilian and Spanish, half-samba, half-flamenco tune on his E♭ clarinet. The fourth plays on his piccolo a march that is half-Scottish, half-Hungarian – more exactly, a Hungarian pentatonic tune that is made to sound like bagpipe music. And the overall harmonic structure is twelve-note. The orchestral accompaniment consists of a three-layered cha-cha, each layer in a different tempo.[4]

(Besides these fakes and misappropriations, there are, Ligeti goes on to note, 'exact quotations in the opera: in scene 2, for instance, the can-can from Offenbach's *Orpheus* is played simultaneously with Schumann's *Merry Peasant*, although I have changed both, adding a verbunkos or Hungarian recruiting song at the end.') Underpinning the 'Collage' is something else: 'All through this passage you can hear, as an ostinato in the bass, the bass subject in the finale of Beethoven's "Eroica" Symphony, but it is transformed into twelve-note music – not quite twelve-note music: there are thirteen notes. It's a parody to start with, but the music becomes in the end quite serious and dignified.'[5]

The medley includes banal fanfares, which eventually take over, and remain to punctuate Nekrotzar's announcement in fuller terms of the coming Doomsday. While there is still time, Astradamors and Piet are all for spending it drinking the wine laid out on the palatial table, and Nekrotzar joins them in an alcoholic trio, he seemingly believing himself to be already drinking human blood. Then he departs into a distracted reverie, accompanied by music of a fantastic rococo sort ('Galimathias', as this section is called in the score, or 'gibberish', being an extension of music that had appeared in the second scene after his encounter with Mescalina) while he recalls his satanic destructions of the past. But the approach of midnight brings him back to his task, and he calls down nothingness as the orchestra slowly marches through a sequence of wide chords, beautiful and ominous. Then, as a canon in the orchestra slips incrementally downwards, he too falls. The end of the world has duly come, but the only one to die is Death himself, to a musical gesture similar to that which had ended the two-piano set. The curtain slowly descends as another dense, still orchestral sequence proceeds.

The fourth scene, or epilogue, has no overture but develops straight out of its predecessor. The setting is the same as for the first scene, 'In the lovely country of Breughelland', where we meet first Piet and Astradamors, who believe themselves to be dead. Before long most of the rest have turned up – Go-Go, Nekrotzar, Mescalina, the Ministers – and when the old sexual and political dissatisfactions begin to fuel dissension, Go-Go orders three ruffians (who arrived on the scene with motorhorn music, hinting that the whole opera belongs to them) to polish off Mescalina and the Ministers. The ruffians also kill the prince, but he almost instantly pops up alive again and decides, with Piet and Astradamors, that since they all feel thirsty they must be still alive. Nekrotzar, dismayed by this turn of events, shrinks and vanishes, to the sound of a quiet chorale-canon for strings. After this second death of Death, 'the sun stands on the horizon in all its glory'. Amando and Amanda emerge from the tomb in which they had been settled throughout two whole scenes, and the orchestra moves into a concluding passacaglia. This is a weird musical rebirth, and it comes as the characters begin to feel that life can go on. Have they really all perished and been resurrected to find themselves in much the same situation? Does the great mystery of death hide nothing more than that everything continues as before? Or was Nekrotzar merely a powerless charlatan? In Ghelderode's play he is shown up as one, but the opera leaves the question open, as Ligeti wanted, and ends with a blithely amoral moral, sung by all the principals:

> Fear not to die, good people all!
> No one knows when his hour will fall.
> And when it comes, then let it be . . .
> Farewell, till then live merrily!

Of course, we hardly need spend two hours in the opera house in order to be told that death will come and meanwhile we might as well enjoy ourselves: the 'message' is as much a false trail as that of *The Rake's Progress*, with which *Le Grand Macabre* shares certain qualities of irony, of reference to other works in the operatic canon (Ligeti has mentioned *Falstaff* and *The Barber of Seville*, as well as the Monteverdi opera, *The Coronation of Poppea*, suggested by the Amando-Amanda duets), of subject matter, of characterization (in particular, Mescalina is an extension of Baba the Turk, quite apart from the inevitable connection between Nekrotzar and Nick Shadow) and of precision engineering. It is a parable, and a parable for an age living posthumously – after the triumph of death brought by the Nekrotzars of totalitarian Europe, and, within the smaller sphere of music, after the obliteration of meaning that had been manifested both by Boulez's total serialism and by Cage's chance procedures. The most important question in such an age has to be that of the reality of these deaths – whether it might still be possible to believe in the value of humanity, whether there could be a future for a species possessing catastrophic means of self-destruction, and whether music would discover, beyond meaninglessness, meaning. Everything Ligeti had composed during the last two decades had been devoted to answering the last question cautiously but affirmatively, which is perhaps also to give a tentative affirmation to the first.

His projection of musical meaning had been made, since 1956, within the postwar modernist stream (if only just within), but of course his growing creation of analogues for traditional means and methods had been to some degree a challenge to modernism. By now, two decades after his joining the Darmstadt-Cologne camp, the avant-garde adventure had lost the energy to sustain itself against such challenges, and *Le Grand Macabre* is of its time in using parody to voice despair: if to go ahead is impossible, to return is worse. For Ligeti, the despair was shortlived and soon regretted: 'In *Le Grand Macabre* I used some quotations, more than allusions, but I now see that as a weakness, a fault, a passing attitude that I don't like and don't want to adopt any more.'[6]

The opera ends, though, optimistically. The final passacaglia, odd as it is and constructedly awkward, seems to promise a new musical dawn, even if at the moment the promise is unsure. According to the composer:

The passacaglia is the only section of the opera that is wholly consonant. The bass subject consists of twelve minor and twelve major sixths: one major and one minor sixth for all twelve notes of the chromatic scale. The resulting twenty-four intervals do not make up a real bass subject; they serve as a frame, which is filled up by major and minor thirds. Consequently you get major and minor chords. All are consonant chords: sweet, almost syrupy, but it is not tonal music . . . My answer to whether it is all parody is that it both is and is not.[7]

There is hope, too, in the whole musical conduct of the drama. *Le Grand Macabre* parades before us a cast of comic-strip exaggerations, but its view of them is amused and benign. Though the whole middleground of operatic behaviour – what one might roughly call 'psychology' – has been bombed out of the score, there is abundant activity at the edges: in music of frenetic speed, speaking a language of onomatopoeia and signal, and in slow, still, glowing passages, whose expressive indications are far more ambiguous. These are the old clocks and clouds of Ligeti's practice, with their parallels in, on the one hand, the *Aventures* pieces and the 'Dies irae' of the Requiem, and, on the other, *Atmosphères* and *Lontano*. The former kind of material, when combined with narrative and generally carrying with it a racket of percussion, suggests cartoon music, while the latter opens the possibility that the opera's burlesque characters also inhabit a far more sophisticated and strange world of feeling and being, as if they were, at the same time, caricatures and gods.

11

After the End of the World

In 1978, the year of the première of *Le Grand Macabre*, Ligeti wrote two short harpsichord pieces, and that was all the music he completed until the Horn Trio four years later. Through the opera he had confronted himself with the end of musical history: the simultaneous availability of multitudinous styles, all of them defunct, with no clear new alternative, the seeming inevitability now of recycling the past. But he would have found the same message in the works of younger composers in Germany, including some who, like Wolfgang von Schweinitz, had been among his Hamburg pupils. And he seems to have discovered it, too, when he sat down at his desk, for a commissioned piano concerto was many times begun and many times abandoned. As he put it in an interview in 1981:

I find myself, so to speak, in a kind of compositional crisis, which, gradually and to some extent furtively, was already opening up during the seventies. And this isn't just a personal crisis but much more, I believe, a crisis of the whole generation to which I belong . . . not to go on composing in an old avant-garde manner that had become a cliché, but also not to decline into a return to earlier styles. I've been trying deliberately in these last years to find an answer for myself – a music that doesn't mean regurgitating the past, including the avant-garde past.[1]

The harpsichord solos are occasional pieces, though distinctly Ligetian ones. They look back over his recent output in that they are both passacaglias, like the last construction in the opera, and both musical machines, like his earlier harpsichord piece, *Continuum*, or the two-piano pieces. They also look further back and at the same time forward, in their explicit rapprochement with Hungary, which the composer was now able to visit again. *Hungarian Rock* is exceedingly fast, founded on a repeating bass of two-two-three-two beats; it emerged as 'a polemical piece in a discussion among my students, some of whom were defending a neotonal pop direction'.[2] As in the opera's passacaglia, the music is saturated with thirds, sixths and triads in disjointed chains, and the freer melody above the ostinato moves through glancing harmonic connections with it, very often supplying the missing note in a triad and then carrying on. This is also an important process in the more sedate *Passacaglia ungherese*, where the two-bar bass – even closer to that of the opera's finale – is constituted entirely of two-note chords, with a melody that plays over the surface, now and then filling in the gaps to make triads. The work was written for an instrument which Eva Nordwall maintained in mean-tone temperament, and this tuning is essential to the harmony, for the piece uses the eight major thirds (and eight corresponding minor sixths) that have the natural frequency ratio of 5:4 and so sound, as Ligeti has put it 'completely clean'.

The silence that followed these harpsichord pieces was broken with the help of a number of new discoveries, which the composer detailed in several interviews and also in his Balzan Prize speech.[3] One was the music of Conlon Nancarrow, who since the early fifties, living in Mexico City, has been composing canons in such intricate cross-rhythms that for many years they could only be realized mechanically, by player pianos. Ligeti came across his music in 1980, and was astonished to find in one of the player-piano studies, no.20, a resemblance to his own *Monument*. It was thanks to his enthusiasm for Nancarrow that the studies were soon afterwards published on compact disc by Wergo. The other stimuli came from a new interest in musical cultures from around the world – especially Brazilian and

Caribbean (for models, again, of cross-rhythm), to which he was introduced by his pupil Roberto Sierra, and later South East Asian (for tuning systems) – and from the revelation of how fractal mathematics could be used to create complex patterns, proceeding by steps that are always logical and elementary towards a magical near-chaos, which had been his procedure in *Continuum* and numerous other pieces. From all these sources, therefore, he gained encouragement to go further along paths already taken, towards polyrhythm, new tunings and algorithmic processes. However, 'the piano concerto produced problems of polyphony, of rhythmic and textural complexity, that I was able to "resolve" in the more reduced instrumentarium of a trio'[4] – an opportunity that arose when the pianist Eckart Besch asked him to write a horn trio. 'As soon as he pronounced the word "horn", somewhere inside my head I heard the sound of a horn as if coming from a distant forest in a fairy tale, just as in a poem by Eichendorff.'[5]

This sounds like an echo not only from Eichendorff but from *Lontano*. However, Ligeti also wanted to say how his new music was different from his old, precisely in connection with the phenomenon of distance: 'I have always liked Schumann, but now he is particularly significant for me. I am trying to change the course of my music, give up the completely cool, distanced music, or rather a music that is as if observed from afar. I want to get it closer to the current, give it immediacy, and in this Schumann's influence on me is considerable.'[6] The work is also inscribed 'Hommage à Brahms' in recognition of the inventor of the horn trio, and certainly it is a lot more traditional in form and voice than the Second String Quartet. For example, there is a clear ternary pattern behind both the first movement (Andantino con tenerezza) and the third (a march plus trio); the music is abundantly motivic; and the instruments have relatively stable characters, not flitting from one kind of playing technique to another.

Other remarks by the composer on his conservatism in this work sound a little defensive:

I really always had, even in the completely wild experimental time, a doubly grounded relationship with tradition. On the one hand, I underwent a very strict traditional schooling at the Budapest Academy of Music. And on the other, in my own music . . . the musical past has constantly played an important role, not on the level of quotation, nor as creative discipline, but rather as aura and allusion. Now the musical language of the Horn Trio is, from a certain viewpoint, different from that of my earlier works: the melodic lines are much more strongly formed as self-sufficient shapes. Yet I think that basically things are as they were in my Second Quartet, in which too the great quartet tradition, obstructed and so half-hidden, was composed with. As model for the formation there is actually only the very, very beautiful work of Brahms. But musically this Horn Trio does not have much to do with my opinions of Brahms; what is remembered from Brahms is perhaps only a certain smilingly conservative comportment – with distinct ironic distance. I think it has much more to do with the late Beethoven, and then more with the music's bearing than with particular compositional-technical procedures. Certainly the piece is based on complex polyphony, on what is, rhythmically and metrically, a very convoluted structure; but to me the primary change is one of bearing, of a bearing that is no longer 'avant-garde'.[7]

Ligeti's problem at this point was to steer a course between modernist cliché and reversionist pastiche, and his solutions came out of the passacaglia of *Le Grand Macabre* and the two little harpsichord pieces, with the assistance of Nancarrow and Caribbean music: a highly constructed music could create patterns rich enough to sustain rather simple ideas, and to justify them in a new way. For instance, the second movement (a Vivacissimo molto ritmico, like *Hungarian Rock*, with which it shares some features) canonically engenders polymetrical combinations of units of three, three and two quaver beats, and small-scale motivic relationships

appear to play on the waves of a powerful rhythmic surge. The
movement is, according to the composer, 'inspired by the various
folk musics of non-existing peoples – that is to say, as if Hungary,
Romania and the entire Balkan region were situated somewhere
between Africa and the Caribbean'.[8] Example 9 shows a passage.
The arrows on the accidentals in the horn part here indicate
microtonal deviations, brought about by the use of natural
harmonics (which occur also, but to a much smaller extent, in the
violin part). The horn thus stands out from its context more
rudely than do the soloists of the Double Concerto: the
instrument is, as it were, syncopated, and the whole piece could
be understood as expressing syncopation in different dimensions.
Cross-rhythm is a vigorous element of the third movement as
well as the second, and the use of triads and other consonances in
contradiction of any tonal stability is a harmonic sort of
syncopation. In concordance with its rhythmic and harmonic
nature, the work is, also, neatly out of step with the orthodox
qualities of form, genre and bearing (to use Ligeti's term) it
seems to embrace. The movements are as elaborately constructed
as those of the two-piano cycle; the difference is that now
facsimiles of traditional features are being constructed.

Another difference is that connections among the movements
are more pronounced: the rhymes are fuller, as Ligeti has
explained.

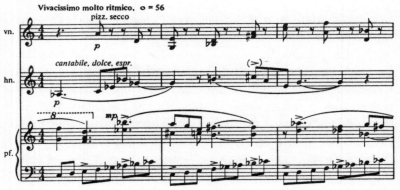

Example 9 From the first movement of the Horn Trio

A major third (G–B) followed by a tritone (E♭–A) and a minor sixth (C–A♭): this descending melodic-harmonic cell – a 'lopsided' variation of the 'horn-fifths' motive – is developed in all four movements . . . While the first three movements are primarily diatonic, the fourth is a chromatic variation of the preceding three, in the guise of a passacaglia. A five-bar harmonic pattern (a variation once again of the horn-fifths cell) provides the framework around which descending chromatic melodic figures increasingly become intertwined, until eventually the five chords are completely overgrown. During this escalation, the piano undergoes a transformation, ultimately emerging as a gigantic imaginary drum, whose echo can be heard in the pedal tones of the horn. A strangely altered reminiscence of the horn-fifths cell appears in the piano and horn, like the photograph of a landscape which in the meantime has dissipated into nothingness.[9]

The large-scale formal reprises of the Trio are a traditional feature Ligeti would not want to meet again, but certainly he had established what he wanted, which was a bridge to 'a new style'. 'I hope I have succeeded – at least for a certain phase of my work – and I now have the feeling that I can work further in this direction.'[10]

12

Choirs New and Old

One great difference between Ligeti's eastern (pre-1956) and western (post-1956) outputs is the comparative lack in the later period of vocal music. Songs and choruses had dominated what he wrote (and even more so what he published) in Budapest, whereas in western Europe his vocal works before 1983 were solitary and exceptional: *Aventures* and *Nouvelles aventures*, the Requiem, *Lux aeterna*, *Clocks and Clouds*, *Le Grand Macabre*. Of course there were practical reasons for such a change. Hungary's musical traditions, its educational system and its political climate all favoured a strong choral culture, which was lacking in the west, and Ligeti himself had participated actively in that culture: 'In my early days in Cluj, and also later as a student in Budapest, I sang a great deal, in choral societies and also in private groups, where we often sang madrigals.'[1] Besides, he must have been disinclined to ask that Hungarian poetry be sung by singers who would not be able to understand it, or even pronounce it properly, and his statements suggest he might have felt that setting German, French or English poetry (all of which he reads) would add a foreign flavour to the goulash of his style – as indeed happened when he came to set texts in German and English. Except for the opera, all his western vocal works hitherto had been in languages either meaningless or dead – or, in the case of *Lux aeterna*, both.

The change in 1983 came with two works for unaccompanied chorus, one to Hungarian poems (*Magyar etüdök*) and one to German (*Drei Phantasien*), written for choirs who had sung and recorded *Lux aeterna* – the Schola Cantorum of Stuttgart and the Swedish Radio Chorus respectively – but stimulated also by feelings of a greater closeness to his homeland (and therefore to his earlier self) that the composer felt with increasing age, and perhaps also with the slow disintegration of the Iron Curtain.

'Now homeland for me,' as he said in talking about the *Magyar etüdök*,

> is something very complex, since I came from Transylvania
> and was brought up speaking Hungarian and partly also
> German. But Transylvania already belonged to Romania at
> the time I was born, and I also learned Romanian, though
> not till later, in secondary school. So where is my
> homeland? . . . I have always felt myself bound in a special
> way to my mother tongue of Hungarian, and now that
> becomes ever more apparent, also in my compositions – not
> only in the choral pieces but also somewhat in the first
> movement of the Horn Trio, where there's a special
> meaning in a particular twist to the musical language that's
> based on Hungarian folklore.[2]

(In connection with the same work, he has also spoken of a folksong character – that of Romanian dirges – in the scalewise descending lament figure on which the finale is based.[3])

Rather as the Horn Trio is a manufactured approach to Viennese chamber music, the *Magyar etüdök* construct a road into the ideal Hungarian village of Bartók and of Ligeti's own pre-1956 choral music. As he has noted of the first number:

> I achieved a very complex musical structure: a canon in
> twelve parts, very strict, in mirror form, six voices going in
> one direction and six in the other. It's neither dodecaphonic
> nor serial, but each voice enters on its own pitch – whence
> the twelve voices. The six ascending voices use the whole-
> tone scale, the six descending ones the same scale a
> semitone higher. The melody is diatonic, but the
> accumulation of voices gradually leads to chromaticism.
> Also, if you look at the score you'll find a canon in
> diminution (in the proportion 2:3). To coordinate the two
> canons at the end, I include silences on one level that are

shifted more quickly. It's truly one of my most 'rigidly calculated' pieces: I wanted to suggest that way the crystalline structure of the ice and the entirely inhuman, mechanical regularity of the process of dripping.

It is, he concluded, 'entirely "automatic," approaching certain constructions of Boulez.'[4]

The allusion must be to *Structures Ia*, perhaps by way of Ligeti's own *Monument*; the earlier icy references are to the text, which, with utmost simplicity, calls to mind the image of a dripping icicle. The simplicity is characteristic of the Weöres poems Ligeti sets: the work's title is the poet's, and implies that these are studies in the Hungarian language as much as Hungarian scenes. Ligeti has described Weöres as 'one of the greatest poets in all world literature',[5] and said how Hungarian 'is very rich in ways of expressing concrete relationships, sensual images – and that with a force and an efficacity above those of Indo-European languages', by virtue of a syntax which 'permits a very great density and a remarkable concision'.[6] His music is similarly concrete, sensual, dense and concise – as it was in the 1955 Weöres setting 'Night', with which the first Hungarian study is comparable in the poetic effect it extracts from canon and clashing modalities.

In the second number, which fields folksong-like strains over sustained phonemes, two texts are combined in the manner of an isorhythmic motet, both of them evocations of sound: sheep bells and the croaking of frogs. The splendid finale is a montage of market cries. 'There are five simultaneous levels, five very simple melodies coordinated harmonically. Each has its own metronome speed, but the tempos have a common denominator that allows synchronization. They are based on the tritone and the whole-tone scale (C♯–D♯–F–G–A–B).'[7] Construction, emphasized by repetition (for each cry is simply reiterated as more and more cries are added), produces a mechanical image of peasant reality, an artificial homeland which is as much as the rootless composer can hope to imagine.

The *Drei Phantasien* are similar to the extent that 'although German texts are set here, the Hungarian a cappella choral tradition is also present in the background'.[8] They are also connected in that Ligeti's primary response is again to imagery:

What particularly ties me to Hölderlin is not so much the immediately linguistic level but much more the pictorial association. Take, for example, a text like the 'Abendphantasiei' . . . This image of the evening sky with purple cloud formations in dying sunlight – unbelievably grandiose, but not pathetic – is connected for me with the conception of one of my favourite pictures, the 'Alexanderschlacht' of Altdorfer in the Munich Pinakothek. The original I only saw later, but as a child I had a reproduction, and the background scenery with golden sunbeams breaking through the blue-grey storm clouds – that was a key experience for me.[9]

(It was so much a key experience that he referred to it also in connection with *Lontano*.[10]) However, the Hölderlin settings are texturally, harmonically and formally more complex than the Weöres group, in keeping with the hugely greater complexity of the verse. The music is more chromatic – even super-chromatic, with microtonal shadings written in – and fiercely demanding too in its use of extreme registers, extreme dynamics and dense micropolyphony. Where the *Magyar etüdök* make complex patterns with simple elements, the *Drei Phantasien* move more chaotically in swirls among sudden intensities and stillnesses.

Alongside this rediscovery of Hungary in new works, Ligeti in the mid-eighties was beginning to take another look at the music he had written before his emigration. Up to this time very little of his early music was known beyond a long sequence of titles: apart from the few works generally available for performance (the First Quartet, *Musica ricercata*, the two Weöres choruses of 1955, the Ballad and Dance for school orchestra), just a few other pieces had received the occasional outing, these including two choral items – the cycle *Idegen földön* and the ballad *Pápainé* – as well as two of a group of three Weöres songs for voice and piano. From 1983 onwards, however, the trickle became a flood, and a large proportion of Ligeti's Hungarian music, mostly short instrumental pieces and choruses, was published during the next decade or so.

The choruses (those Ligeti has rescued being all unac-companied) are close to folksong, whether they be arrangements, resettings of traditional texts or settings of poems by modern writers in folk style. Such, of course, were the conditions of Hungarian culture during the decade after 1945, but the folksong language was also one that Ligeti had long been familiar with: 'One reason for my interest in folklore,' he has said, 'is also bound up with the fact that I knew it from childhood: I heard it; our cook sang it.'[11] Of course, the resurrected choruses of 1946–53 are much simpler than the new ones that appeared at the same time, being diatonic and almost always in two, three or four parts rather than sixteen (though *Pápainé*, texturally the most complex piece before the 1955 pair, goes in for striking chromaticism as it tells of the widow's murder at the hands of nine robbers, and perhaps distantly recalls the blunt narration of brutal events in *Le Grand Macabre* – another 'ballad', as Ghelderode called it). Nevertheless, the basic means of canon and modality are the same, and there are echoes across the years, as may be suggested by Example 10, which brings together melodies from *Pápainé* and the second of the *Magyar etüdök*, both showing trochaic rhythm, a rising fourth and a falling tetrachord. (Falling tetrachords and other modal descents are among the folksong features refracted through the harsh glass of sophistication in the isolated Hölderlin song 'Der Sommer' of 1989, set for soprano and piano.) The phase of forgetting – of forgetting which was partly self-forgetting – was over, and Ligeti in his sixties was discovering he was still the same man he had been in his youth, only more experienced, more adept and more free.

Example 10 From the second of the Magyar etüdök *(a) and* Pápainé *(b)*

What happens when homely elements are set upon by a high intelligence is often the art of nonsense, and the *Magyar etüdök* are nonsense music in the same way that the Weöres poems are nonsense verse: the meaning is supremely in the form. A commission for the King's Singers obliged Ligeti to think again in terms of simple choral textures (in six parts, for two altos, tenor, two baritones and bass), and for the texts he turned to nineteenth-century English nonsense poetry to make six Nonsense Madrigals (1988–93). The techniques are those of his post-opera style – interlocked ostinatos, chorales in contradictory consonances, canons – coupled with cute dialogues and arch quotation ('The farther off from England the nearer is to France', a line from 'The Lobster Quadrille', slips from one national anthem into the other). Best of the set is the one without words, a setting of letter names in alphabetical order as a characteristic slow-moving harmonic cloudscape.

13

(An Imaginary Opera)

The completion of the Horn Trio in 1982 left Ligeti with two major tasks: the Piano Concerto, which had been waiting for some years, and a second opera, commissioned that year by the English National Opera and the BBC. His first idea for the opera, on which he began serious work in the year of the Horn Trio, was to make a version of *The Tempest*; Geoffrey Skelton, who had translated *Le Grand Macabre* for the ENO production of that year, was to draw a libretto from the play. Progress, however, was slow, and in the early nineties the project was dropped in favour of a musical dramatization of the *Alice* books, leaving *The Tempest* as a fascinating possibility documented most fully by the composer's enticing description of how the prelude might have sounded:

The first sketches for the prelude to my (future) opera after Shakespeare's *The Tempest* begin with an (as it were) monodic, very fast melody, which is not really monodic but made by a complex mixture-sound. In other words, many parts run in rhythmic synchrony, and blend into a governing 'part', whose sound spectrum is made sometimes from harmonic overtones, sometimes from a composed noise structure, but chiefly from the transition from one sound state to another. A harmonic spectrum is gradually changed in colour – the partials are so placed – that bell-like sounds arise, and then slowly pass into coloured noises . . . What then happens to the mixture melody in the further course of the *Tempest* prelude is influenced by the thought-world of iterative calculus and recursive structures. The melodic line becomes, so to speak, multiplied with itself, like the endless reflections that result when one sees oneself between two parallel mirrors. I used such a multiplication procedure earlier in the fourth movement of my Piano Concerto, there in the form of a whirlpool, whose eye was gradually, spirally reached by the formal process. (I worked too with the mixture melodies for the first time in this movement.) In the *Tempest* prelude there's no whirlpool (created in the Piano Concerto by the diminution of a recurrent melody), but instead an increasing branching of the melodic lines, so that the original monodic melody is gradually transformed into a complexly pulsating musical 'space'. (What thereby results is a highly stylized musical suggestion of a sea storm, with 'frozen' turbulences: the very rapid rhythmic movement appears static, as if time stood still.)[1]

The *Tempest* sketch described here must date from 1987 – the year in which the fourth movement of the Piano Concerto was finished and the essay quoted here was published – and might have been influenced (in the monody of complex sounds) by Ligeti's recent discovery of the music of Claude Vivier, as well as by those larger presences that loom behind his other works of this period: Nancarrow and fractals. Further traces of the vanished *Tempest* can be found among his other statements. For example, the world of the court was to be defined by baritones and basses, that of Caliban by counter-tenors and tenors (perhaps with the unsettling shrillness that distinguishes Ligeti's writing for the counter-tenor voice in *Le Grand Macabre* and the Nonsense Madrigals), and this 'semi-barbarous' territory of Caliban's was to be staked out also by complex polyrhythm. Also, the composer was concerned that his second opera avoid the conventionality that, with hindsight, he saw in his first – even in the staging he most admired, which was that of the 1979 Bologna production, with designs by Roland Topor: 'That was marvellous because it was really a black piece, demoniac, exceedingly bizarre, savage, cruel.'[2]

14

Pianos Old and New

Some compensation for the loss of *The Tempest* comes in the works from this period that did see the light of day: the long-delayed Piano Concerto (1985–8) and the continuing sequence of Etudes for piano. As in the choral sphere, Ligeti at the keyboard was discovering things he had known for decades, and the appearance of the first book of Etudes (1985) coincided with the reappearance of three pieces from 1947–8 made into a triptych: Capriccio no.1 (a short sonata movement), Invention, and Capriccio no.2. Qualities of the Etudes are here foreshadowed, within a still Bartókian style: lucidity of harmony, polyphonic texture, simplicity of basic element (but not the complexity of process that makes each of the Etudes a virtuoso feat of composition as well as a pianist's showpiece) and, in Capriccio no.2, the play of figures on a moto perpetuo ground. Other works from this short postwar, pre-Stalinist phase in Hungarian history similarly have a light inventive freedom that seems then to have been unavailable to the composer until the time of *Musica ricercata*: the Three Weöres Songs of 1946-7, for instance, are lively with patterns made from a few notes and from rhythmic alterations. However, this is the Etudes' prehistory; Ligeti's more continuous output of piano than of choral music allows for closer parallels with the manic systematization of the *Monument* cycle and with how the piano works in the Horn Trio.

It is reassuring, of course, to find some continuity of style through the works of fifty years, but one of the essential lessons of Ligeti's music is that, just as any particular work has to be made, so tradition itself is a construct, and one that a composer will alter. The Etudes are unthinkable without the example of his earlier piano music, but they are even more unthinkable without the recent entries to his personal pantheon: the example of Nancarrow and – to indicate how Nancarrowesque polyrhythm might be performable by a solo musician – that of African music. (His huge enthusiasm for new musical discoveries – an enthusiasm continuing into his seventies – is not only an engaging aspect of his personality but a real benefit to his own music's development.) 'In African music,' he has said,

> there is a ground layer consisting of fast, even pulsations which are, however, not counted as such but rather felt, and an upper layer of occasionally symmetrical but more often asymmetrical patterns of varying length, though always even multiples of the basic pulse. That which is eminently new in my piano Etudes is the possibility of a *single* interpreter being able to produce the illusion of *several* simultaneous layers of different tempi. That is to say, our perception can be outwitted by imposing a 'European' accent pattern on to the non-accentuated 'African' pulsation.[1]

The first Etude, 'Désordre', offers, as Denys Bouliane has shown,[2] an exemplary demonstration of polymetric process, of synthesis from elements drawn out of different musical cultures, and of growth from a set of ad hoc ideas and rules, most of which are stated or implicit in the opening bars, reproduced in Example 11. This algorithmic way of working is Ligeti's inheritance from the computer age. After the Cologne experience he never went back to electronic composition, and his feeling for musical craftsmanship is such that he could never have, like Xenakis, profited from abstract calculation; what he deduced from computers was rather – and more deeply – new ways to think musically, 'It's a question of adopting a "generative" kind of compositional thinking, where basic principles function in the manner of genetic codes in the unfolding of "vegetal" musical forms.'[3]

'Désordre' is such a musical plant. The principal idea is a melody in three segments, of four, four and six bars, and this is

Example 11 Opening of Etude no.1 'Désordre'

subjected to various rules, as follows. It keeps changing its mind about whether it has three-plus-five or five-plus-three quavers in each bar. Unused quaver beats are filled with scale patterns, so that the melody, initially going at a quick but not immoderate pace, is placed in a hectic moto perpetuo. Where the right hand plays only on the white keys, the left plays only on the black. The left hand doubles the right, but because it is working in a five-note mode rather than a seven-note one, its intervals are larger. (This rule is subject to a lot of exceptions, which perhaps have to do with other aims Ligeti has for his harmony. For example, the interval between the two hands in the first segment of the melody is always a minor sixth, tritone or major third, whereas in the second segment the minor third replaces the minor sixth. However, one of the sources of 'disorder' in the piece is the lack of agreement between harmony and rhythm: see the next rule.) The two hands slip out of synchrony in a manner that is at first organized – the right hand skips a quaver every fourth bar – but later becomes more chaotic (as, indeed, so much in the music becomes more chaotic as it makes its journey upwards and offwards). The melody is repeated fourteen times, moving up a scale degree each time. From the fourth repetition to the tenth, a process of compression sets in, until by the tenth the notes of the melody are almost indistinguishable from those of the scalar infill.

Many of the features of this study – the withdrawal of figure into ground, the manic but precisely mechanical activity, the intimations of processes which are never fully revealed, or which go astray – can be traced back quite clearly to *Monument – Selbstportrait – Bewegung*, and even, a little less clearly, to *Continuum*. Most especially, the image of disorder – self-declared by the study – is thoroughly Ligetian. It is striking that in so much of his music, including every one of the Etudes, order is unsustainable: organization disintegrates, and rules become, through repeated application, weapons with which the structure attacks itself. No doubt he was stimulated in the eighties by the new prominence in scientific thinking of theories concerning chaotic and complex events, but he had been creating his own chaotic and complex events since at least *Apparitions*, and his dynamic of disorder had a history going back to the metronome piece. The intuition that order leads to chaos did not need to come out of his scientific reading; it could well, though, have been strengthened by his experience of living with political and musical regimes.

What is new in the Etudes, or at least very much increased, is the acceptance of diatonic figures and chords outside of any tonal frame, and the exactly analogous acceptance of rhythmic groupings with no stable metrical frame: in making these their chief distinguishing features, the Etudes assume a key role in Ligeti's later music. In the particular case of 'Désordre', the initial tonal ambiguity could be phrased thus: is the right-hand melody in the Aeolian mode on A or in the Locrian on B? Unable to make up its mind, the melody takes a step upwards. In just the same way – and this may be easier to appreciate in a short extract – certainties about accent or metre keep changing too, and the influence of Nancarrow is evident not just in the mad-machine sound world (which Ligeti had long had as his own) but in the liveliness and awkwardness of the polymetre and in the engineered acceleration. The music is in a marvellously organized confusion, which it has made inevitable, seemingly of itself, by its basic premises.

The other five studies in the first book share the basic features of 'Désordre': 'generative' construction from simple elements, imprints from folk music, harmony and metre in states of bewilderment or veiling, novel musical processes that come from the nature of the instrument – as in the third, 'Touches bloquées', which develops in a more intensive way the blocked-key technique of *Selbstportrait* to make gapped rhythms in a right-hand moto perpetuo that moves over keys silently depressed by the left. The titles of the pieces may, as in this case, be indications of how they were made, or they may be metaphors of poetic effect: 'Désordre', 'Fanfares', 'Cordes à vide', 'Arc-en-ciel'.

Not only the titles but the iridescent uncertainties of harmony and rhythm place the studies within the ambit of Debussy (of his studies but also of his preludes, among which 'Feux d'artifice' is one of the most Ligetian pieces composed before Ligeti was born), whose music is particularly evoked by the more diatonic pieces. 'Cordes à vide' is a study in fifths: hence the reference to open strings. 'Fanfares' places its heraldic musical pronouncements – in thirds, sixths, fifths and triads – on a rapid ostinato of three-two-three beats, and as in 'Désordre' compound metre provides manifold opportunities for cross-rhythm between the hands. As in 'Désordre' too, there is cross-harmony, between the unchanging, dark ostinato and the light fanfares, whose chords are built around the ostinato's notes. To quote Richard Steinitz: 'The whirl of these many harmonic ingredients around the rotating spindle of the ostinato sets up centrifugal forces, as harmonies are spun outwards above and below the centre, at times flying off to extremities.'[4]

The title of the finale to the first book of Etudes, 'Automne à Varsovie', alludes to the Warsaw Autumn festival that had been one of the main showcases for contemporary music since the mid-fifties, to the hazardous political and economic condition of Poland in the early eighties, and to the presence here, as in *Selbstportrait*, of Chopin. In explaining his new polyrhythm as an extension of classical hemiola (the ambiguity in 6/8 metre between two units of three beats and three of two), Ligeti cited Chopin and Schumann as forebears,[5] and Chopin is recalled too in the almost continuous semiquaver arpeggiation of 'Automne à Varsovie'. Against this even stream the music moves mostly in descending chromatic scales, which are superposed in up to four layers going at different speeds: at one point, for instance, there are scales whose notes occur at intervals of four, five and seven semiquavers (though with certain notes given double duration), 'like tired labourers returning home, united in resignation and only distinguishable by the speed of their gait',[6] treading a path similar to that taken in the finale of the Horn Trio. As Steinitz has pointed out in the same article, the slowly descending chromatic scale was

used as a passacaglia bass by baroque composers, such as
Monteverdi and Purcell, for great laments: part of the ominousness
of this music comes out of the absence of anything above the bass,
which supports only smaller or larger versions of itself.

The first book of Etudes, depending so much on musical qualities particular to the piano (rapid rhythmic regularity, precision of
attack to define metre, highly controlled polyphony), seems to
have provided Ligeti at last with a route into his Piano Concerto
(1985–8), which had been on the stocks for a decade before it was
completed. Some information about one earlier state of the
concerto is recorded in an interview the composer gave in 1981,
when clearly he was already heading in the right direction:
'What's important is a great rhythmic complexity, an overlaying
of many different metric levels – what Ives began and later
Nancarrow consistently developed further; also, there was
something of that in my Chamber Concerto. I'm going further in
this direction, and so working with musical shapes that have
harder, sharper rhythmic contours than in my earlier works.'[7] But
other references – to a Schumannesque 'cross between an
interior, luxuriant ornamental style and craziness', or to the first
and third movements being both 'unruly, unrestrained pieces'
with the marking 'agitato appassionato' – conjure images slightly
different from those of the eventual work.

Support for the necessity of the Etudes as a gateway might come
from the presence of three super-Etudes in the concerto as its odd-
numbered movements, all of them requiring the piano to play
almost constantly and generally to provide a background of
figuration against which – or out from which – melodies appear
elsewhere on the keyboard and in other instruments, taking on lives
of their own. As in the Etudes, the piano seems to be working as an
imagination machine, a machine manufacturing the music on the
spot, and the first movement is close to 'Désordre', even if the
presence of orchestral instruments – a deliberately mistuned horn,
as in the Trio; piccolo and later other woodwind playing something
like a folk dance – produces a much less single-minded result, as

well as a much more colourful one.

In the other two movements the piano is more a partner. The second begins, over a double-bass pedal, with a canon of mostly minor-second descents in piccolo, bassoon, slide whistle, piano, brass and ocarina, the unconventional instruments here introducing their own wayward intonations. Out of this the piano extends a chorale, whose elements are greeted and imitated by the orchestra with varying degrees of amusement and frenzy. (The Piano Concerto is surely a comic work, but also a scary one.) The fourth movement is, Ligeti has said, 'a fractal piece', where 'the principle of construction is a certain geometric vortex: the ever-decreasing rhythmical values produce the sensation of a kind of acceleration.' At first the events are spaced out, with intervening silences, but they recur in altered form at shorter and shorter intervals (this is easiest to spot in the case of the opening gesture) and are often extended, so that time gets more and more filled, and more and more confused. At a point beyond where even the keenest ear's bewilderment must be complete, the movement fades away.

Ligeti went straight on from the concerto to the second book of Etudes, originally planned on the Debussy model to contain another six pieces,[8] of which the first three were composed between 1988 and 1990. Other works then supervened – the Violin Concerto and the beginnings of the Viola Sonata – and when he returned to the Etudes in 1993–4 he added not three but five more to the second book. All eight pieces in this book are, to the extent that this is possible, more frenetic than the six of the first, with only the fifth, 'En suspens', offering any prolonged relief from incessant activity. The opener to the new book – 'Galamb borong', whose title juxtaposes two Hungarian words to make fake Indonesian – has the two hands playing in different whole-tone scales to summon echoes of gamelan music. Next comes 'Fém' (Metal), whose Hungarian title, as Ulrich Dibelius has pointed out,[9] allows for suggestions of 'Fény' (Light), an idea that recurs – surely prompted by the light of open harmony and natural resonance intensified by speed – in Ligeti's music of this time: the finale of the Piano Concerto is a Presto luminoso and the first movement of the Violin Concerto a Vivacissimo luminoso, which is also the marking on 'Galamb borong'. 'Fém' is a hocket in even rhythmic values, alternately loud and soft, locked into close registral spaces, and moving from fifths and triads to more complex chords: the sound is harsh, clangorous, indeed metallic, and indeed also luminous. In a quiet coda, some of the territory is gone over again at one-third speed.

The occasional reductive coda only points up how, like those of the first book, the new Etudes generally move in the direction of increasing complexity and disorder as a result of the piling-up of material and the escalating effect of built-in 'mistakes'. 'Vertige', the third piece in the second book, provides a relatively straightforward instance. The material consists of sprays of fast downward chromatic scales, which at first are copies of one another occurring at regular intervals (so that the music stays in the same place on the keyboard), but that soon begin to drift in initial point, to alter in timing and to change in length. In the background there seems to be the ideal of a perfect chromatic homogeneity, in which all twelve notes are equal and each leads on only to its neighbour below. But this ideal is unattainable: the scales have to start and finish somewhere, and these endpoints will gain undue importance; also, the superpositions of scales may produce diatonic intervals and even triads, as indeed happens. There can be no lack of differentiation. Out of the grey flow, coloured items will emerge, and Ligeti is soon helping them do so – highlighting melodies and chords by means of accent and lengthened duration.

Etude no.10, 'Der Zauberlehrling' (The Sorcerer's Apprentice), is a scherzo, a *Continuum* for piano in which a simple ostinato is constantly on the move rhythmically and harmonically, turning at the main crisis point into an A♭ Phrygian scale. Next comes 'En suspens', which sounds like an attempt to remember Debussy's 'Clair de lune', and after that 'Entrelacs'. In both these studies the hands again have non-overlapping sets of keys: five black plus one white (a different choice in each study, defining a different harmonic colour), and the six white remaining. 'Entrelacs' has figures that emerge from the broken reflections of them contained in the mobile fluid of perpetual semiquaver tremolandos and arpeggios.

The study placed in the sinister thirteenth position, 'L'escalier du diable' (The Devil's Staircase), is the most imposing and alarming of all. Its stairs are chromatic steps, in rising scales, braided as the falling scales of 'Vertige' had been. But this time the movement is hobbled. Each scalar note is divided from the next by one or two foreign notes, which are at first chosen from a whole-tone scale, but which soon may be elements in other rising chromatic progressions; so there are units of two or three notes, and these are assembled in expanding-contracting patterns (2-2-3 – 2-2-2-3 – 2-2-3 – 2-2-2-3 – 2-2-2-2-3 – 2-2-2-3, and so on). After a page of this furious, driven but irregular music, the right hand terrifyingly breaks free, but is still bound into chromatic-scale figures, played as runs are harmonized to make slow chords. The inexorable upward stairways seem to be able to continue for ever, because when one of them reaches the top of the keyboard another two or more will still have room ahead, but eventually both hands are crammed into the far treble and the uneven steppings stop. Chords now appear alone, as if peering around in an emptied musical space, but the rule of upward chromatic motion soon reasserts itself and, despite the wild ringing of bells, the music returns towards its former condition, compelled to go on rising.

Ligeti had begun the piece that turned into 'L'escalier du diable' with the intention that it should be the concluding sixth number in the second book, and that it should be very different from the corresponding piece in the first book, 'Automne à Varsovie'. It already had a title – a relic from the *Tempest* project: 'The isle is full of noises, sounds and sweet airs' – and the isle was to be 'a little like Debussy's *L'isle joyeuse*: the whole

instrument sounds like a large orchestra, and it's a paradise'.[10]
Ligeti's explanation for the lapse of this optimistic prospect is in
terms of his experience in Los Angeles, where he spent some
weeks in the early part of 1993 on the occasion of the American
première of his Violin Concerto, shocked by violently stormy
weather and by the extremities of wealth and poverty he saw
around him. As he points out in the same interview, 'L'escalier du
diable' shows on the one side 'geometry and construction', with
on the other 'the most unrestrained, extreme emotion'. Of course,
these are two sides of the same coin – for compulsive ascent is
both the work's central, terrifying affect and its structural
mechanism – but that must mean also that the composer's choice
of what geometry to work with is influenced by his state of mind.

After writing 'L'escalier du diable' Ligeti added on a new
finale, and then inserted 'Der Zauberlehrling' to bring the total in
the second book to eight. He soon decided that his first version of
the concluding study, 'Coloana fără sfârşit', was too difficult for
a living pianist (though the possibility remains . . .) and so produced a somewhat simplified replacement, 'Coloana infinită',
which is still hugely challenging and hugely impressive as a
turmoil of energy pushing, again, upwards. The title's allusion is
to an immense column of metal created by Brancusi, which is no
doubt a suitable metaphor for music of such monumental and
implacable presence. In total contrast, 'White on White' begins
the third book of Etudes with a slow chorale-canon entirely on
the white keys in the treble register, though out of these restricted
means come harmonic inclinations that are crooked and unstable,
as so often in late Ligeti slow movements: progressions (in this
case triads are rare, and chords are generally unrepeated) often
seem to be pulling in two or more directions at the same time.
The piece then turns into a typical play of asymmetrical melody
on asymmetrically grouped running quavers, but still only on the
white notes until very near the end.

15

Strings Tuned and Retuned

Ligeti's output in his sixties and seventies resembles that of his twenties in the prominence not only of choral and piano works but of music for strings. On a different plane there is the connection that in both periods – though not in the interim – he was working in the context of traditions outside that of western classical music: Central European folk music in the decade up to 1955, and that plus countless worldwide musical cultures in the eighties and nineties, his statements of this period including references to music from the Caribbean, sub-Saharan Africa, Indonesia, Burma, the Solomon Islands, New Guinea, the Bismarck Islands, etc. His broadening of reference – coupled with a constancy of perspective, which is perhaps rooted in the need to reconstruct any borrowings, to understand his music from the ground up, and to justify variety in terms of some generative principle or formal idea – would be obvious from a comparison of, say, the Capriccios and Invention with the second book of Etudes, and so it is with his rather smaller but latterly crucial repertory of music featuring solo strings.

The most important of the early string pieces he resurrected in the eighties and nineties is the Sonata for solo cello, which is in two movements: 'Dialogo' (a love song of 1948, distinguished by Hungarian-style melody and a beautiful pizzicato glissando effect) and 'Capriccio' (added in 1953, a moto perpetuo with reference to the first movement's melody). He found it easier to write for the cello than for other string instruments because he had learned the instrument at the conservatory in Cluj;[1] later there was also the stimulus of cellist friends, among them Siegfried Palm, for whom he wrote his first concerto. When the request for a concerto came from Saschko Gawriloff, the violinist in the first performance of the Horn Trio, he felt the need for some self-education: 'I read everything about violin technique and, as I always do, intensely studied the instrument's literature. My models were Paganini, the Bach solo sonatas, Ysaÿe's solo sonatas, Wieniawski and Szymanowski. This however did not replace the missing inner tactile image of feeling the strings under my fingers.' (He had just been speaking of the Etudes and the Piano Concerto, where 'the sensual impression of feeling the keyboard under my fingers became part of the imagination for the music.') 'I could never "touch" the violin, never really feel the position changes.'[2]

Perhaps this untouchability is expressed in the otherworldliness of the piece, which takes place so much in the upper treble, as if the music were levitating, and in which the composer pursues, much further than before, his fascination with new and rival tunings. He had made experiments with the DX7 synthesizer, but had become fed up with the artificial sound quality and tried retuning the harp (to a scale of seven equal intervals per octave, with the pedals allowing chromatic transposition) and harpsichord. 'Finally I gave up on both instruments, realizing that I was entering a harmonic labyrinth so complicated that I was getting lost in it. Perhaps later I shall go right through it some time (it isn't endless).'[3] He turned instead to a chamber orchestra with a few more wind players than that of the Piano Concerto but a considerably smaller body of strings. As in the Piano Concerto, the brass sometimes play natural harmonics and there are instruments of uncertain intonation (ocarinas, slide whistles, recorder); in addition, one violin and one viola from the orchestra are tuned to harmonics on the double bass. 'First, the double-bass player . . . produces the seventh harmonic on the G string, which is a low F, that is to say, a "perfect" minor seventh . . . The violinist tunes his E string to this . . . and adjusts the other strings in the usual fifths accordingly. In this way, every string of his violin will sound a narrow minor second higher compared to the other violins.'[4] Similarly, the

viola's D string is tuned to the lowered C♯ the bass produces as
fifth overtone on the A string. These tunings of these instruments
(A♭–E♭–B♭–F and B–F♯–C♯–G♯), together with those of their
normal companions, thus provide a cycle of fifths in just
intonation, and provide for the most delicate abrasions between
equal temperament and natural resonance.

The interview cited here was conducted in the summer of
1990, by which time Ligeti had completed only the first
movement of the first version of the concerto. This movement
was subsequently abandoned (except that Gawriloff used
stretches of the solo part to make a cadenza for the finale of the
work's second, definitive version), but the scordatura violin and
viola were retained, as were the frequent string harmonics. These
– in the fine-spun textures of the new first movement, where
melodies and mechanisms in elaborate polymetres characteristically evolve out of, and sink back into, trills – contribute to
what the composer has aptly described as a 'glassy shimmering
character' and 'the expression of fragility and danger'.

Where the Piano Concerto had one slow movement, placed
off-centre, the Violin Concerto has two, in second and fourth
positions among its five movements, so that there is a Bartókian
symmetry. The fourth movement (originally the second) is a
passacaglia whose ground bass defines itself principally in
chromatic-scale fragments winding upwards through the
orchestra; the second has a tripartite title, 'Aria, Hoquetus,
Choral', to suggest how a slow melody, played by the soloist
alone at the start, gains contrapuntal interruptions and harmonic
reinterpretations (notably from faltering ocarina quartet and a
brass section also mouldering with mistuned harmonics). The
tune is an odd one by any standards but Ligeti's, being diatonic
but unable to settle into any stable key or metre – a folksong for
the homeless.

Echoes of a desperate nostalgia recur in the later movements,
cross cut with the wonder of fabrication and discovery conveyed
by this extraordinary work, which could well have assumed the

Shakespearian title of the unachieved study: 'The isle is full of noises'. In the interlude between the slow movements (a piece that was originally the finale), the soloist plays a melody that seems to arise as a rainbow from the interference between the light of sustained tones, including those of the retuned violin and viola, and the showering of chromatic scales. Then in the eventual finale it is as if all the charms and strangenesses of the preceding movements were being multiplied on top of each other, until the soloist is bumped off by the orchestra in a gesture as brutal and comic as the killings in *Le Grand Macabre*.

The composition of the concerto, extending over four years, overlapped with work on the second book of Etudes, the Nonsense Madrigals and the Sonata for solo viola, as well as perhaps with the decision to abandon *The Tempest* and create a 'revue or musical' on the *Alice* books – a project first mentioned in April 1993, when the composer recorded the interview in Ulrich Dibelius's book.[5] The Sonata is another book of Etudes – of pieces that are manifestly constructed, that demand virtuoso performance, and whose images are at once strongly determined and fiercely expressive, their geometry human. However, Ligeti's contemplation of an unaccompanied string player (someone therefore in a very different position from that of the concerto's soloist) resulted in a work unlike any other in his output: close again to Central European folk music, but dislocatedly so, close also to Bach in its polyphonic conception, necessarily simple in texture, and yet packing on to one stave a rich complexity of disparate harmonic, rhythmic and formal purposes.

Most folkish is the first movement, whose title of 'Hora lungă' refers to a Romanian style identified by Bartók. In this style 'the third and fourth degrees are frequently fluctuating, neutral sounds, roughly half-flat or half-sharp'[6] – a practice Ligeti follows by asking for special fingerings of these notes, and also of the seventh; since the piece is performed entirely on the C string and stays within a compass of two octaves (except for occasional ladders of natural harmonics), the retuning is realistic.

Ligeti also imitates his model in making his melody out of formulae which the piece separately develops, and in enjoying rhythmic freedom. But this is not pastiche. In particular, the grave tune is unsure quite which note to gravitate towards: F, C or G.

'Loop', the second movement and first to be written, sounds more like a folk dance, alternating bars of eight beats (usually 5+3) and ten (usually 2+2+3+3), and revelling in all the possibilities of syncopation. The 'loop' is a chain of forty-four double stops, whose durations are progressively shortened: at its first appearance, after an initial run through just the first four chords, the loop occupies thirty-seven crotchets; at its ninth and last, now going in almost continuous semiquavers, it is all done in twelve. 'Facsar' (Wring), which follows, is also based on a repeating unit of forty-four items: this time a melody whose rhythmic profile is preserved until very near the end, but which gains an increasing density and acerbity of accompanying harmony and counterpoints. Example 12 shows this melody as it first appears, uncomplicated, though with the internal complication of wave and tonality so typical of Ligeti. The tune is full of self-similarities (most notably, the last bar is identical with the third, up a fourth) and of similarities to the first movement, but there is no decisive final or tonic, and the line moves on easily – another loop – into a repetition of itself. Being harmonically polyvalent, it will accept all kinds of harmonic interpretation: the progress of the piece therefore becomes, very characteristically, an unpacking of what is inherent in the basic material.

The fourth movement, 'Presto con sordino', is a wave machine of even quavers played as fast as possible (which will be more or less fast, and the quavers more or less even, depending on the changes of fingering that are needed). After this, the 'Lamento', all in multiple stops, cuts between ferocious fortissimo interjections and distant pianissimos, these related to the 'horn fifths' of the Horn Trio and latterly played in harmonics. The finale brings together, as its title of 'Chaconne chromatique'

**Andante cantàbile ed espressivo,
with swing,** ♪ *ca.* **116**

Example 12 Opening of the third movement, 'Facsar', of the Viola Sonata

implies, two recurrent machines in later Ligeti: a repeating ground bass (here classically in eight bars of triple time) and the chromatic scale. As usual, the development is towards increasing disorder that arrives out of, not in contradiction to, the initial order. From one falling chromatic scale others branch out until, as in the third movement, the fact of repetition is concealed within thickets of power and fury.

Eliminating the possibility of harmonies of resonance – realized directly in the Etudes for piano and in the metallophone and percussion sounds of the Violin Concerto, and indirectly in the finely teased wind-string chords of the latter work – the Viola Sonata withdraws from Caribbean-African-Asian-Pacific territory towards a European homeland. However, this is a momentary gambit. Ligeti's music of the eighties and nineties explores crucial issues of identity across a field so vast that, one might think, identity must crumble. Yet it does not. In an age when so many composers have limited themselves to a narrow line, whether of continuing modernism or of a minimalism of some kind, Ligeti has opened himself further and further to the music of the world: to everything in the western classical tradition from Machaut to Claude Vivier (both admitted influences on the Violin Concerto[7]), and to a huge range of musical cultures from around the world. At the same time, his thinking has taken account of intuitions into, and metaphors of, mental workings that have come to us from computers. Those intuitions and metaphors might suggest that the individual is defined less by style than by process, and certainly it would be difficult to give an account of Ligeti's style that would happily embrace, say, *Atmosphères* and the Viola Sonata. In terms of inquisitive, fundamental-seeking, exploratory process, though, and of reaction (usually surprising and contradictory) to the world around him, he has been for half a century the same man, and his ability to be himself, even while greeting so much around him (and abhorring only laziness and half-measures), can only make us all optimistic.

Notes

Part One: East
Interview with the Composer
1 The third has been reconstructed from the composer's sketches by Fred Sallis. Many other works unpublished in 1983 have also since appeared.

Part Two: West
1 Pierre Michel, *György Ligeti: Compositeur d'aujourd'hui*, p. 139.
2 Ibid.
3 Ibid., p. 146.
4 Ibid., p. 145.
5 *Ligeti in Conversation*, p. 34.
6 Ibid., p. 87.
7 See Michel, op. cit., p. 139.

1 *News from Hungary*
1 'Neue Musik in Ungarn', *Melos* (1949).
2 'Neues aus Budapest: Zwölftonmusik oder "Neue Tonalität"?', *Melos* (1950).

2 *A New Atmosphere, and* Atmosphères
1 Ove Nordwall, *György Ligeti: Eine Monographie*, p. 41
2 'Zustände, Ereignisse, Wandlungen' (written in 1960, published in *Melos* in 1967).

3 *Ligeti in Conversation*, p. 33.
4 The movement is to all intents and purposes published in the composer's essay 'Spielanweisungen zur Erstfassung des zweiten Satzes der "Apparitions"', *Musica* (1968).
5 See Michel, op. cit., p. 146.
6 Letter of 17 April 1966, in Nordwall, op. cit., p. 36.

7 Michel, op. cit., pp. 149–50.
8 'Metamorphoses of Musical Form' (1958, published in *Die Reihe*, 1960, 1965).
9 Michel, op. cit., pp. 149–50.
10 Ibid., p. 148.
11 Ibid., p. 156.
12 *Ligeti in Conversation*, p. 101.
13 Michel, op. cit., p. 141.
14 Ibid., p. 151.
15 'Über neue Wege in Kompositionsunterricht', *Three Aspects of New Music* (1968), p. 13.
16 *Ligeti in Conversation*, p. 85.
17 Ibid., p. 51.

3 *Adventures, and* Aventures
1 See Nordwall, op. cit., p. 7.
2 Note with Wergo 60161.
3 *Ligeti in Conversation*, p. 17.
4 Michel, op. cit., pp. 158–9.
5 Note with Wergo 60045.
6 Nordwall, op. cit., pp. 75–6.
7 *Ligeti in Conversation*, p. 45.
8 Nordwall, op. cit., p. 49.
9 Letter of 10 August 1966 in Nordwall, op. cit., p. 79.
10 Letter of 7 February 1967 , ibid., pp. 79-84.
11 *Ligeti in Conversation*, p. 60.
12 Michel, op. cit., p. 153.
13 Ibid., pp. 178–9.
14 Note with Wergo 60163.
15 Letter of 7 February 1967 in Nordwall, op. cit., pp. 79–84.

4 *Requiem*
1 *Ligeti in Conversation*, p. 48.
2 Ibid., p. 47.
3 Ibid.

4   Ibid., p. 49.
5   Ibid., p. 53.
6   Ibid., p. 49.
7   Ibid., p. 20.
8   Michel, op. cit., p. 154.
9   Ibid., p. 161.
10 Ibid., p. 130.
11 Ibid., p. 162.

5   *Harmonies*
1   Letter of 22 February 1967 in Nordwall, op. cit., p. 87.
2   For an analysis of the work, see Jonathan W. Bernard, 'Voice
    Leading as a Spatial Function in the Music of Ligeti', *Music
    Analysis*, xiii, 1994.
3   Michel, op. cit., p. 161.
4   *Ligeti in Conversation*, pp. 98–9.
5   Letter of 22 February 1967 in Nordwall, op. cit., p. 87.
6   *Ligeti in Conversation*, p. 126.
7   Ibid., p. 93.
8   Ibid., p. 22.
9   Letter of 19 February 1968 in Nordwall, op. cit., p. 92.
10 *Ligeti in Conversation*, p. 61.
11 Kolleritsch (ed.), *György Ligeti: Personalstil – Avantgard-
    ismus – Popularität*, p. 96. Two years after this symposium
    took place he was to plant his first book of Etudes in similar
    earth, but that work was still undreamt of.

6   *Four and Five*
1   'Auf dem Weg zu "Lux aeterna"', 1969.
2   *Ligeti in Conversation*, pp. 107–9.
3   The composer accepts this interpretation in his interview with
    Stephen Satory, *Canadian University Music Review* x1, 1990,
    pp. 101–7.
4   *Ligeti in Conversation*, p. 109.
5   Ibid., pp. 50–51.

6   Letter of 5–6 August 1968 in Nordwall, op. cit., p. 93.
7   Ibid., p. 96.
8   Michel, op. cit., p. 148.
9   Letter of 6 November 1968 in Nordwall, op. cit., p. 108.
10 Michel, op. cit., p. 132.
11 I am grateful to Bálint András Varga for help in interpreting the Hungarian text.

7   *Ramifications*
1   Nordwall,, op. cit., p. 113.
2   Ibid., pp. 109–13.
3   *Ligeti in Conversation*, p. 64.

8   *Melodies*
1   *Ligeti in Conversation*, pp. 54–5.
2   Ibid.

9   *Clocks and Clouds and Polyphonies*
1   Stürzbecher, Werkstattgespräche mit Komponisten, 1971.
2   Michel, op. cit., p. 175.
3   Note with Wergo 60163.
4   *Ligeti in Conversation*, p. 44.
5   Ibid., pp. 66–7.
6   For a detailed analysis of the whole triptych, see Stephen Ferguson, *György Ligetis Drei Stücke für Zwei Klaviere: Eine Gesamtanalyse*, 1994.
7   See Michel, op. cit., p. 173.
8   See his 'Neue Wege der Klaviertechnik', *Melos* x1 (1973), pp. 143–6.

10 Le Grand Macabre
1   'Zur Enstehung der Oper "Le Grand Macabre"', 1978.
2   In 1966 Ligeti completed a thorough revision, in which cuts were made to the text, the orchestration was much revised, the roles of Black and White Ministers, originally spoken,

were set to music, and the final passacaglia gained a somewhat longer ending.

3 *Ligeti in Conversation*, p. 69.
4 Ibid., p. 59.
5 Ibid., p. 69.
6 Interview with Denys Bouliane, 1983.
7 *Ligeti in Conversation*, p. 70.

11 After the End of the World
1 Interview with Monika Lichtenfeld, 1981.
2 Kolleritsch (ed.), *György Ligeti: Personalstil – Avantgardismus – Popularität*, p. 95.
3 'Rhapsodische, unausgewogene Gedanken über Musik, besonders über meine eigenen Kompositionen', 1993.
4 Interview with Denys Bouliane, 1983.
5 *Ligeti in Conversation*, p. 22.
6 Ibid., p. 78.
7 Interview with Monika Lichtenfeld, 1984.
8 Note with ECD 75555.
9 Ibid.
10 Interview with Monika Lichtenfeld, 1984.

12 Choirs New and Old
1 Interview with Monika Lichtenfeld, 1984.
2 Ibid.
3 Interview with Denys Bouliane, 1983.
4 Ibid.
5 Ibid.
6 Ibid.
7 Ibid.
8 Interview with Monika Lichtenfeld, 1984.
9 Ibid.
10 *Ligeti in Conversation*, pp. 92–3.
11 Michel, op. cit., p. 129.

13 *(An Imaginary Opera)*
1 'Computer und Komposition'.
2 Interview with Edna Politi, 1985.

14 *Pianos Old and New*
1 Note with ECD 75555.
2 '"Six Etudes pour piano" de György Ligeti', *Contrechamps*, no. 12–13 (1990), pp. 98–132.
3 'Ma position comme compositeur aujourd'hui', 1990. See also 'Computer und Komposition'.
4 Richard Steinitz, 'The Dynamics of Disorder', *Musical Times*, 1996.
5 See note with ECD 75555.
6 Richard Steinitz, 'The Dynamics of Disorder'.
7 Interview with Monika Lichtenfeld, 1981.
8 See the interview with Tünde Szitha.
9 In Dibelius, *György Ligeti: Eine Monographie in Essays*, p. 231.
10 Interview with Ulrich Dibelius.

15 *Strings Tuned and Retuned*
1 See note with DG 431 813.
2 Duchesneau, 'György Ligeti on his Violin Concerto', *Ligeti Letter* no. 2, 1995.
3 Interview with Tünde Szitha.
4 Ibid.
5 Dibelius, *György Ligeti: Eine Monographie in Essays*, p. 272.
6 'Hora lungă', *The New Grove*.
7 See Duchesneau, 'György Ligeti on his Violin Concerto'.

List of Works and Recordings

Works that the composer considers juvenilia, not meriting performance, are noted as such by obelisks. Most of these pieces are unpublished. All other works are published by Schott, with the exception only of those from the composer's first decade outside Hungary, when his publishers were Universal (1958–61) and Peters (1962–6). Editions from these houses, and from various Hungarian and Romanian publishers in the years before 1956, are indicated. First-performance details are introduced by asterisks, and information about recordings by bullets: solid in the case of LPs, open for CDs. Dates when recordings were made are given where known.

Induló [March] (1942) and *Polifón etüd* (1943) for piano duet, 3 min.
  o   Sony SK 62307 (Pierre-Laurent Aimard, Irina Kataeva, 1995)

†   Cantata no.1 'Et circa horam nonam' (Latin liturgical text) for mezzo-soprano soloist, two choruses and instruments (1944–5)

†   *Burját-Mongol aratódal* [Buriatic-Mongolia Harvest Song] for chorus (1945) (CGS, Cluj)

†   *Dereng már a hajnal* [The Dawn's Already Rising] (Balázs Fodor) for chorus (1945) (Józsa Béla Athenaeum, Cluj; Cserépfalvi, Budapest)

†   Cantata no.2 'Venit angelus' (Latin liturgical text) for mezzo-soprano soloist, chorus and instruments (1945)

† Three Attila József Choruses (1945)

† Duo for violin and cello (1945)

† *Bicinia biciae* (József, traditional, textless), seven duos for SBar or chorus (1945)
no.IV: *Betlehemi királyok* [The Magi] (József) for two-part mixed or women's chorus (1946), 1½ min.
* London Sinfonietta Voices/Terry Edwards, Gütersloh, 24 April 1994
o Sony SK 62305 (musicians of première, 1994)

† *Kis szerenád* [Little Serenade] for string orchestra (1945, revised 1947)

Idegen földön [Abroad] for women's chorus (1945–6), 3¼ min.
I. Siralmas nékem [Misery Me] (Bálint Balassa) (1945) – II. Egy fekete holló [A Dark Raven] (Hungarian traditional) (1945) – III. Vissza ne nézz [Once the Forest] (Hungarian traditional) (1945) – IV. Fujdogál a nyári szél [The Summer Wind Blows Gently] (Slovak traditional, trans. Belá Balázs) (1946)
* Swedish Radio Chorus/Eric Ericson, Stockholm, 17 April 1971
o Sony SK 62305 (London Sinfonietta Voices/Terry Edwards, 1994)

Húsvét [Easter] (Hungarian traditional) for two women's choruses (1946), 2 min.
* London Sinfonietta Voices/Terry Edwards, Gütersloh, 24 April 1994
o Sony SK 62305 (musicians of première, 1994)

Magány [Solitude] (Sándor Weöres) for chorus (1946), 2½ min.
* Schola Cantorum Stuttgart/Clytus Gottwald, Stuttgart, 18 May 1983
o EMI CDC 7 54096 (Groupe Vocal de France/Guy Reibel, 1988); o Sony SK 62305 (London Sinfonietta Voices/Terry Edwards, 1994)

Bujdosó [Wandering] (Hungarian traditional) for chorus (1946), 2 min.
- o EMI CDC 7 54096 (Groupe Vocal de France/Guy Reibel, 1990); o Sony SK 62305 (London Sinfonietta Voices/Terry Edwards, 1994)

Magos kősziklának [By the Huge Rock] (Hungarian traditional) for chorus (1946), 2 min.
- * London Sinfonietta Voices/Terry Edwards, Gütersloh, 24 April 1994
- o Sony SK 62305 (musicians of première, 1994)

† Duo for violin and piano (1946)

Three Songs (Weöres) for soprano and piano (1946-7), 5 min. I. Táncol a hold [The Moon Dances] (1947) – II. Gyümölcsfürt [Bunch of Fruit] (1947) – III. Kalmár jött nagy madarakkal [The Merchant Came with Large Birds] (1946)
- * Edith Gáncs/Ligeti, Budapest, 1947; first performance outside Hungary, of nos.I and II: Dorothy Dorow/Liisa Pohjola, Junsele, Sweden, 23 July 1970
- o Sony SK 62311 (Rosemary Hardy, Pierre-Laurent Aimard, 1996)

Two Capriccios (XI and V–VI 1947) and Invention (i. 1948) for piano, 2¼ min., 1¼ min., 1¾ min., (in published order: Capriccio no.1 – Invention – Capriccio no.2)
- * Márta and György Kurtág, Budapest, 1948
- o Wergo 60131 (Begoña Uriarte, Karl-Hermann Mrongovius, 1985); o Col Legno 031 815 (Erika Haase); o Sony SK 62307 (Irina Kataeva, 1995); o Sony SK 62310 (Pierre Charial *barrel organ*, 1995); o BIS 783 (Fredrik Ullén, 1996)

Ha folyóvíz volnék [If I Could Flow Like the River] (Slovak traditional in Hungarian translation), four-part canon for voices (1947), 1 min. (Zeneműkiadó, as no.127 of *165 Kánon* ed. Péter József)

* London Sinfonietta Voices/Terry Edwards, Gütersloh, 24 April 1994

o Sony SK 62305 (musicians of première, 1994)

† *Nagy idök* [Great Times] (Sándor Petöfi) for four-part chorus (1948)

† *Mifiso la sodo* for small orchestra (1948)

† *Bölcsötöl a sírig* [From the Cradle to the Grave] (Hungarian traditional) for soprano, mezzo-soprano, oboe, clarinet and string quartet (1948), 25 min.

* Budapest Radio, 1948

† *Ifjúsági kantáta* [Cantata for Youth] (Péter Kuczka) for four soloists, four-part chorus and orchestra (1948-9)

* student soloists, chorus and orchestra of the Franz Liszt Academy/Carl Melles, Budapest, 1949

Régi magyar társas táncok [Old Hungarian Parlour Dances, Alte ungarische Gesellschaftstänze] for string orchestra with flute and/or clarinet ad lib. (1949), 12 min. (Zeneműkiado, Schott)
I. Andante – II. Allegro – III. Andantino maestoso – IV. Allegro moderato

* Budapest Radio, 1949

o Sony 62318 (Philharmonia/Esa-Pekka Salonen, 1995)

† *Tavaszi virág* [Spring Flower] (Zoltán Körmöczi), music for a puppet play, for seven singers and chamber ensemble (1949)

* Budapest Puppet Theatre, 1949

Baladă şi joc [Ballad and Dance, Ballade und Tanz] for school orchestra or two violins (1950), 3 min.
I. Andantino – II. Allegro vivace, energisch
orchestral version: treble rec(s), perc, pf, vns, vcs, dbs ad lib.

* school orchestra from Győr/Frigyes Sándor, Budapest, 1950

o Sony SK 62306 (Irvine Arditti, David Alberman, 1994)

Andante cantabile and Allegretto poco capriccioso for string
quartet (1950), 7 min.
* Arditti Quartet, Salzburg, 28 July 1994
o Sony SK 62306 (Arditti Quartet, 1994)

† Three Attila József Songs for voice and piano (1950)
* Edith Gáncs/Ligeti, Budapest, 1950

† *Román népdalok és táncok/Cântece poporane româneşti*
[Romanian Folk Songs and Dances] for mezzo-soprano and
baritone soloists with small orchestra (1950)
* Budapest Radio, 1950

† *Petőfi bordala* [Petőfi's Drinking Song] (Petőfi) for voice
and piano (1950) (Zeneműkiadó)

Kállai kettős [Kálló Two-Step] (Hungarian traditional) for chorus
(1950), 2³/₄ min. (Zeneműkiadó)
* Chorus of the State Security/József Gát, Budapest, 1950
o EMI CDC 7 54096 (Groupe Vocal de France/Guy Reibel,
1990); o Sony SK 62305 (London Sinfonietta
Voices/Terry Edwards, 1994)

† *Tél* [Winter] (Weöres), two pieces for chorus (1950)

Négy lakodalmi tánc [Four Wedding Dances] (Hungarian
traditional) for three women's voices and piano (1950), 4
min. (Zeneműkiadó)
I. A menyasszony szép virag [The Bride is a Lovely Flower]
– II. A kapuban a szekér [The Cart is at the Gate] – III. Hopp
ide tisztán [Come Quickly Pretty One] – IV. Mikor kedves
Laci bátyám . . . [When My Dear Uncle Laci . . .]
* Budapest Radio, 1950
o Sony SK 62311 (Rosemary Hardy, Eva Wedin, Malena
Ernman, Pierre-Laurent Aimard, 1996)

Három lakodalmi tánc [Three Wedding Dances, Drei Hoch-
zeitstänze] for piano duet, arranged from nos. II–IV of the
above (1950), 2¹/₂ min. (Zeneműkiadó)

* Begoña Uriarte, Karl-Hermann Mrongovius, Schloss Hohenems, 2 August 1986
o Sony SK 62307 (Pierre-Laurent Aimard, Irina Kataeva, 1995)

Lakodalmas [Wedding Dance] (Hungarian traditional) for chorus (1950), 1 min. (Zeneműkiadó)
o EMI CDC 7 54096 (Groupe Vocal de France/Guy Reibel, 1990); o Sony SK 62305 (London Sinfonietta Voices/Terry Edwards, 1994)

Sonatina for piano duet (1950–51), 4½ min.
I. Allegro (arranged from no.III of *Musica ricercata*) – II. Andante (arranged from no.VII of *Musica ricercata*) – III. Vivace
* Begoña Uriarte, Karl-Hermann Mrongovius, Schloss Hohenems, 2 August 1986
o Sony SK 62307 (Pierre-Laurent Aimard, Irina Kataeva, 1995)

† *Grande sonate militaire* op.69 for piano (1951), orchestrated as *Grande symphonie militaire* op.69a (1951)

† *Középlokon esik az eső* [It's Raining in Középlok] (Hungarian traditional) for voice and piano (1951) (Zeneműkiadó)

† *Az asszony és a katona* [The Woman and the Soldier] (Hungarian traditional) for chorus (1951) (Zeneműkiadó)

Hortobágy (Hungarian traditional) for chorus (1951) (Zeneműkiadó)
* Soroksár Chorus/Zoltán Simon, Budapest, 1951
o Sony SK 62305 (London Sinfonietta Voices/Terry Edwards, 1994)

Concert Românesc [Romanian Concerto] for orchestra (1952), 14 min.

I. Larghetto – II. Allegro vivace – III. Adagio ma non troppo
– IV. Presto
2.2.3.2 – 3.2.0.0 – perc – strings
o   Sony SK 62318 (Philharmonia/Esa-Pekka Salonen, 1996)

Five Songs (János Arany) for voice and piano (1952), 10 min.
I. Csalfa sugár [False Hope] – II. A legszebb virág [The
Loveliest Flower] – III. A csendos dalokból [From the Quiet
Songs] IV. A bujdosó [The Errant] – V. Az ördög elvitte a
fináncot [The Devil Abducted the Taxman]
o   Sony SK 62311 (Rosemary Hardy, Pierre-Laurent
Aimard, 1996)

Haj, ifjúság! [Youth] (Hungarian traditional) for chorus (1952), 3
min.
*   M.T. Központi Együttes Énekkarra/Árpád Darázs,
Budapest, 1952
o   EMI CDC 7 54096 (Groupe Vocal de France/Guy Reibel,
1990); o   Sony SK 62305 (London Sinfonietta
Voices/Terry Edwards, 1994)

Pletykázó asszonyok [Gossip] (Weöres), four-part canon for
voices (1952), 1¹/₂ (Zeneműkiadó, as no.128 of *165 Kánon*
ed. Péter József)
o   EMI CDC 7 54096 (Groupe Vocal de France/Guy Reibel,
1990); o   Sony SK 62305 (London Sinfonietta
Voices/Terry Edwards, 1994)

Sonata for cello solo (1948–53), 8³/₄ min.
I. Dialogo: Adagio, rubato, cantabile – II. Capriccio: Presto
con slancio
*   Manfred Stilz, Paris, 24 October 1983
o   DG 431813 (Matt Haimovitz, 1990); o   Sony 62315
(David Geringas, 1995)

Musica ricercata for piano (1951–3), 23 min.
I. Sostenuto – II. Mesto, rigido e cerimoniale – III. Allegro
con spirito – IV. Tempo di valse (poco vivace – 'à l'orgue de

Barbarie') – V. Rubato: Lamentoso – VI. Allegro molto
capriccioso – VII. Cantabile, molto legato – VIII. Vivace:
Energico – IX. Adagio: Mesto (Béla Bartók in memoriam) –
X. Vivace: Capriccioso – XI. Andante misurato e tranquillo
(Omaggio a Girolamo Frescobaldi)
* Liisa Pohjola, Sundsvall, Sweden, 18 November 1969
o BIS 53 (Liisa Pohjola, 1974); o Wergo 60131 (Begoña
  Uriarte, Karl-Hermann Mrongovius, 1985); o Col Legno
  031 815 (Erika Haase); o Sony SK 62310 (Pierre Charial
  barrel organ, 1995); o Sony SK 62308 (Pierre-Laurent
  Aimard, 1996)

Sonatina for piano duet (1950-51), two movements arranged
from nos. III and VII: *see above*
Six Bagatelles for wind quintet, arranged from nos.III, V,
VII–X (1953), 12¹/₂ min.
I. Allegro con spirito – II. Rubato: Lamentoso – III. Allegro
grazioso – IV. Presto ruvido – V. Adagio: Mesto (Béla Bartók
in memoriam) – VI. Molto vivace: Capriccioso
* Stockholm Philharmonic Wind Quintet, Malmö, 20
  January 1969
o EMI 763 8672 (musicians of première); ● Deutsche
  Harmonia Mundi 2013 (Albert Schweitzer Quintet); o
  Bayer 100 052 (Calamus Ensemble); o Crystal 750
  (Westwood Quintet); o Ambitus 97 887 (Roseau Quintet);
  o Valois 4639 (Quinette Moragues, 1991); Sony SK 48052
  (Ensemble Wien Berlin); o BIS 662 (Berlin Philharmonic
  Wind Quintet, 1994); o Ermitage 418 (Quintetto
  Bibicona, 1995); o Sony SK 62309 (London Winds, 1995)

Ricercare: Omaggio a Frescobaldi for organ, arranged from
no. XI (1953), 5 min.
o Sony SK 62307 (Zsigmond Szathmáry, 1995)

Inaktelki nóták [Songs from Inaktelke] (Hungarian traditional)
for chorus (1953) (Zeneműkiadó)

* London Sinfonietta Voices/Terry Edwards, Gütersloh, 24
April 1994
o Sony SK 62305 (musicians of première, 1994)

Pápainé [Widow Pápai] (Hungarian traditional) for chorus
(1953), 3 min.
* Swedish Radio Chorus/Eric Ericson, Stockholm, 16 May
1967
o EMI CDC 7 54096 (Groupe Vocal de France/Guy Reibel,
1988); o Sony SK 62305 (London Sinfonietta
Voices/Terry Edwards, 1994)

String Quartet no.1 'Métamorphoses nocturnes' (1953–4), 21
min.
* Ramor Quartet, Vienna, 8 May 1958
o BIS 53 (Voces Intimae Quartet, 1976); o Wergo 60079
(Arditti Quartet, 1978); o DG 431 686 (Hagen Quartet); o
Sony SK 62306 (Arditti Quartet, 1994)

Mátraszenimrei dalok [Songs from Mátraszentimre] (Hungarian
traditional) for chorus (1955), 5 min.
I. Három hordó [Three Barrels] – II. Igaz szerelem [True
Love] – III. Gomb, gomb [Button] – IV. Erdőbe, erdőbe [In
the Forest]
* Hagen Chamber Choir/Robert Pappert, Saarbrücken, 9
June 1984
o EMI CDC 7 54096 (Groupe Vocal de France/Guy Reibel,
1990); o Sony SK 62305 (London Sinfonietta
Voices/Terry Edwards, 1994)

Éjszaka [Night] and *Reggel* [Morning] (Weöres) for chorus
(1955), $2^3/_4$ min. and $1^1/_4$ min.
* Stockholm Radio Choir/Eric Ericson, Stockholm, 1970
● EMI 129 916 (musicians of première); o EMI CDC 7
54096 (Groupe Vocal de France/Guy Reibel, 1988); o
Sony SK 62305 (London Sinfonietta Voices/Terry
Edwards, 1994)

† *Chromatische Phantasie* for piano (1956), 5 min.

Glissandi on one-track tape (v–viii.1957), 7¹/₂ min.
o   Wergo 60161

Pièce électronique no.3 on four-track tape (xi.1957–i.1958), realized by Kees Tazelaar at the Conservatory of The Hague (1996), 2 min. (Schott: draft)
*   The Hague, 2 February 1996
o   Sony SK 62318

Artikulation on four-track tape (i–iii. 1958), 3³/₄ min. (Schott: 'Hörpartitur' by Rainer Wehinger)
*   West German Radio, 25 March 1958
o   Wergo 60161; o Sony SK 62318

Apparitions for orchestra (1958-9), 9 min. (Universal)
I. Lento – II. Agitato
3.0.3.3 – 6.3.3.1 – cel, harp, hpd, pf, 4 perc – 12.12.8.8.6, plus three violins and trumpet offstage
*   North German Radio Symphony Orchestra/Ernest Bour, Cologne, 19 June 1960
o   Sony SK 62316 (Philharmonia/Esa-Pekka Salonen, 1997)

Atmosphères for orchestra (ii–vii.1961), 9 min. (Universal)
4. 4. 4. 4 – 6. 4. 4. 1 – pf – 14.14.10.10.8
*   South West German Radio Symphony Orchestra/Hans Rosbaud, Donaueschingen, 22 October 1961
o   Col Legno AU 031 800 (studio recording made soon before première); o Wergo 60162 (South West German Radio Symphony Orchestra/Ernest Bour, 1966); • Columbia MS 6733 (New York Philharmonic Orchestra/Leonard Bernstein); o Colosseum 34 47 253 (Yomiuri Nippon Symphony Orchestra/Seiji Ozawa); o DG 429 260 (Vienna Philharmonic Orchestra/Claudio Abbado, 1988); o Sony SK 62316 (Philharmonia/Esa-Pekka Salonen, 1997)

Die Zukunft der Musik [The Future of Music] for lecturer and audience (viii. 1961), 10 min. (in *Dé/Collage* no.3, Cologne, 1962)
* * Ligeti and audience, Alpbach, Tyrol, August 1961

Trois bagatelles for pianist (viii. 1961), free duration (Fluxus)
* * Karl-Erik Welin, Wiesbaden, 26 September 1962

Fragment for ten players (x. 1961, rev. 1964), 7–10 min. (Universal)
cbn, b trbn, b tuba, harp, hpd, pf, perc, 3 db
* * Munich Philharmonic Orchestra members/Ligeti, Munich, 23 March 1962

Volumina for organ (xii. 1961–i. 1962, rev. iv–v. 1966), 16 min. (Peters)
* * Karl-Erik Welin, Bremen, 4 May 1962; same player, Kiel, 8 March 1968 (revised version)
* o Wergo 60161 (Karl-Erik Welin, 1962); ● Candide-Vox CE 31009 (Gerd Zacher); o DG 2530 392 (Gerd Zacher); ● Da Camera Magna 93237 (Zsigmond Szathmáry); ● Christophorus SCK 70 350 (Werner Jacob); o Sony SK 62307 (Zsigmond Szathmáry, 1995)

Poème symphonique for a hundred metronomes (xi. 1962), 20-30 min.
* * Hilversum, 13 September 1963
* ● Edition Michael Frauenlob Bauer MFB 008 (1989); o Sony SK 62310 (1995)

Aventures (v.–xii. 1962) and *Nouvelles aventures* (1962– xii. 1965) for three singers and seven players, 11 min. and 12½ min. (Peters)
coloratura S, A, Bar; fl (pic), hn, hpd, pf (cel), perc, vc, db
* * Gertie Charlent, Marie-Thérèse Cahn, William Pearson, Die Reihe/Friedrich Cerha, Hamburg, 4 April 1963 (*Aventures*); same soloists, North German Radio Symphony Orchestra members/Andrzej Markowski,

Hamburg, 26 May 1966 (*Nouvelles aventures*)
o Wergo 60045 (both works: same soloists, Darmstadt International Chamber Ensemble/Bruno Maderna, 1966); • Candide-Vox CE 31009 (both works: musicians of *Aventures* première, 1968); o DG 423 244 (*Aventures* only: Jane Manning, Mary Thomas, William Pearson, Ensemble InterContemporain/Pierre Boulez, 1981); o Sony SK 62311 (both works: Phyllis Bryn-Julson, Rose Taylor, Omar Ebrahim, Philharmonia/Esa-Pekka Salonen, 1995)

Aventures and Nouvelles aventures (i–ii. 1966)
stage version of both works with libretto by Ligeti
* soloists of concert premières, Stuttgart Opera Orchestra members/Friedrich Cerha, production by Rolf Scharre, Stuttgart, Staatstheater, 19 October 1966

Requiem for soloists, choruses and orchestra (spring 1963–i. 1965), 27 min. (Peters)
I. Introitus – II. Kyrie – III. De die judicii sequentia – IV. Lacrimosa
solo S, solo Mez, two choruses; 3.3.3.3–4.4.3.1–cel, harp, hpd, 3 perc–strings
* Liliana Poli, Barbro Ericson, Swedish Radio Chorus and Orchestra/Michael Gielen, Stockholm, 14 March 1965
o Wergo 60045 (same soloists, Bavarian Radio Chorus, Hesse Radio Symphony Orchestra/Michael Gielen, 1968); o Sony SK 62316 (Sibylle Ehlert, Charlotte Hellekant, London Sinfonietta Voices, Philharmonia/Esa-Pekka Salonen, 1996)

Lux aeterna for sixteen voices (vii–viii. 1966), 8½ min. (Peters)
* Schola Cantorum Stuttgart/Clytus Gottwald, Stuttgart, 2 November 1966
o Wergo 60162 (musicians of première, 1966); • EMI 1 C 063 29075 (Stockholm Radio Chorus/Eric Ericson); o DG

423 244 (North German Radio Chorus/Helmut Franz, 1968); ● Columbia MS 7176 (Gregg Smith Singers); o EMI CDC 7 54096 (Groupe Vocal de France/Guy Reibel, 1988); o Sony SK 62305 (London Sinfonietta Voices/Terry Edwards, 1994)

Cello Concerto (vii.–xii.–1966), 16 min. (Peters)
I. crotchet – 40 – II. Lo stesso tempo
solo vc; 1.1.2.1 – 1.1.1.0 – harp.8.7.6.5.4 (or 1.1.1.1.1)
* Siegfried Palm, Berlin Radio Symphony Orchestra/Henryk Czyz, Berlin, 19 April 1967
o Wergo 60163 (Siegfried Palm, Hesse Radio Orchestra/Michael Gielen, 1967); o Sony SK 58945 (Miklós Perényi, Ensemble Modern/PeterEötvös, 1990); o DG 439 808 (Jean-Guihen Queyras, Ensemble InterContemporain/Pierre Boulez, 1992); o Sony SK 62315 (David Geringas, Philharmonia/Esa-Pekka Salonen, 1996)

Lontano for orchestra (v. 1967), 11 min.
4.4.4.4 – 4.3.3.1 – strings
* South West German Radio Symphony Orchestra/Ernest Bour, Donaueschingen, 22 October 1967
o Wergo 60163 (studio recording from time of première); o DG 429 260 (Vienna Philharmonic Orchestra/Claudio Abbado, 1988); o Sony SK 62317 (Philharmonia/Esa-Pekka Salonen, 1997)

Continuum for harpsichord (1968), 4 min. or less
* Antoinette Vischer, Basle, October 1968
o Wergo 60161 (Antoinette Vischer); o BIS 53 (Eva Nordwall, 1976); o Wergo 60100 (Elisabeth Chojnacka, 1983/4); o Col Legno 031 815 (Erika Haase); o Finlandia 367 (Jukka Tiensuu); o Sony SK 62307 (Elisabeth Chojnacka, 1995); o Sony SK 62310 (Pierre Charial *barrel organ*, 1995)

String Quartet no.2 (iii.–v. 1968), 21½ min.
I. Allegro nervoso – II. Sostenuto, molto calmo – III. Come un meccanismo di precisione – IV. Presto furioso, brutale, tumultuoso – V. Allegro con delicatezza
* LaSalle Quartet, Baden-Baden, 14 December 1969
o DG 423 244 (LaSalle Quartet, 1969); o Wergo 60079 (Arditti Quartet, 1978); o Sony SK 62306 (Arditti Quartet, 1994)

Ten Pieces for wind quintet (viii.–xii. 1968), 14–15 min.
I. Molto sostenuto e calmo – II. Prestissimo minaccioso e burlesco – III. Lento – IV. Prestissimo leggiero e virtuoso – V. Presto staccatissimo e leggiero – VI. Presto staccatissimo e leggiero – VII. Vivo, energico – VIII. Allegro con delicatezza – IX. Sostenuto, stridente – X. Presto bizarro e rubato, so schnell wie möglich
* Stockholm Philharmonic Wind Quintet, Malmö, 20 January 1969
o EMI 763 8672 (musicians of première); o Wergo 60161 (South West German Radio Wind Quintet); o Decca 425 623 (Vienna Wind Soloists, 1976); o ART 007 (Fifth Species); o Stradivarius STR 33304 (Arnold); o BIS 662 (Berlin Philharmonic Wind Quintet, 1994); o Ermitage 418 (Quintetto Bibicona, 1995); o Sony SK 62309 (London Winds, 1995)

Two Studies for organ: *Harmonies* (vii. 1967) and *Coulée* (vii. 1969), 6–9 min. and 3½ min.
* Gerd Zacher, Hamburg, 14 October 1967 (*Harmonies*); Gerd Zacher, Seckau Basilica, 19 October 1969 (*Coulée*)
• DG 137 003, 2530 392, 2543 818, Candide-Vox CE 31009 (*Harmonies* only: Gerd Zacher); • Christophorus SCK 70 350 (*Harmonies* only: Werner Jacob); • Cantate 658 229 (*Harmonies* only: Peter Schumann); o Wergo 60161 (both studies: Zsigmond Szathmáry); o Sony SK 62307 (both studies: Zsigmond Szathmáry, 1995)

Ramifications for solo strings 7.0.2.2.1 or string orchestra (xii. 1968–iii. 1969), 8½ min.

* Berlin Radio Symphony Orchestra/Michael Gielen, Berlin, 23 April 1969 (orchestral version [1]); Saar Radio Chamber Orchestra/Antonio Janigro, Saarbrücken, 10 October 1969 (chamber version [2])
o Wergo 60162 (1: South West German Radio Symphony Orchestra/Ernest Bour, 1970; 2: musicians of première, 1970); ● EMI C 061 11316 (2: Toulouse Chamber Orchestra/Auriacombe); o Polyphonia Köln 881 204 (1: Junge Solisten Saarbrücken/Michael Luig); o DG 423 244 (2: Ensemble InterContemporain/Pierre Boulez, 1982); o Col Legno AU 31842 (2: Collegium Musicum/Timur Mynbaev, 1989); o Sony SK 62317 (Philharmonia/Esa-Pekka Salonen, 1997)

Chamber Concerto for thirteen players (1969–70), 20 min.
I. Corrente – II. Calmo, sostenuto – III. Movimento preciso e meccanico – IV. Presto
1.1.2.0 – 1.0.1.0 – hpd (Hammond org), pf (cel) – 1.1.1.1.1
* Die Reihe/Friedrich Cerha, Berlin, 1 October 1970
● Hungaroton 11807 (Budapest Chamber Ensemble/András Mihály); o Wergo 60162 (musicians of première); o Decca 425 623 (London Sinfonietta/David Atherton, 1975); o DG 423 244 (Ensemble InterContemporain/Pierre Boulez, 1982); o Sony SK 58945 (Ensemble Modern/Peter Eötvös, 1992); o UMMUS 102 (Lorraine Vaillancourt); o Sony SK 62317 (Philharmonia/Esa-Pekka Salonen, 1997)

Melodien for orchestra (1971), 12–13 min.
1.1.1.1. – 2.1.1.0 – pf (cel), perc – 8.7.6.5.4 (or 1.1.1.1.1)
* Nuremberg Philharmonic Orchestra/Hans Gierster, Nuremberg, 10 December 1971
o Decca 425 623 (London Sinfonietta/David Atherton, 1975); o Sony SK 62317 (Philharmonia/Esa-Pekka Salonen, 1997)

Double Concerto for flute, oboe and orchestra (1972), 15 min.
  I. Calmo, con tenerezza – II. Allegro corrente
  solo fl (a fl/b fl), solo ob; 3.3.3.3 – 2.1.1.0 – cel, harp, keyed
  perc (glock, vib, xyl) – 0.0.4.6.4
  * Karlheinz Zöller, Lothar Koch, Berlin Philharmonic
    Orchestra/Christoph von Dohnányi, Berlin, 16 September
    1972

  o Wergo 60163, BIS 53 (Gunilla von Bahr, Thorleif
    Lännerholm, Swedish Radio Symphony Orchestra/Elgar
    Howarth, 1975); o Decca 425 623 (Aurèle Nicolet, Heinz
    Holliger, London Sinfonietta/David Atherton, 1975); o
    Sony SK 62316 (Emmanuel Pahud, Heinz Holliger,
    Philharmonia/Esa-Pekka Salonen, 1997)

Clocks and Clouds for female chorus and orchestra (1972–3), 13
min.
  4 S, 4 Mez, 4 A; 5.3.5.4. – 0.2.0.0 – cel, glock, vib, 2 harps –
  0.0.4.6.4
  * Austrian Radio Chorus and Symphony Orchestra/
    Friedrich Cerha, Graz, 15 October 1973
  o Sony SK 62317 (London Sinfonietta Female Chorus,
    Philharmonia/Esa-Pekka Salonen, 1997)

San Francisco Polyphony for orchestra (1973–4) 10½ min.
  3.3.3.3 – 2.2.2.1 – harp, pf (cel), perc, keyed perc (glock, vib,
  xyl) – strings
  * San Francisco Symphony Orchestra/Seiji Ozawa, San
    Francisco, 8 January 1975
  o Wergo 60163, BIS 53 (Swedish Radio Symphony
    Orchestra/Elgar Howarth, 1975); o Sony SK 62317
    (Philharmonia/Esa-Pekka Salonen, 1996)

Monument – Selbstportrait – Bewegung for two pianos (ii.–iv.
1976), 15 min.

  I. Monument – II. Selbstportrait mit Reich und Riley (und
  Chopin ist auch dabei) – III. In zart fliessender Bewegung

* Alfons and Aloys Kontarsky, Cologne, 15 May 1976
• DG 2531 102 (musicians of première); o Wergo 60100 (Antonio Ballista, Bruno Canino, 1983/4); o Wergo 60131 (Begoña Uriarte, Karl-Hermann Mrongovius, 1985); o Sony SK 62307 (Pierre-Laurent Aimard, Irina Kataeva, 1995)

Rondeau for actor and tape (1976)
* Wolfgang Höper, Stuttgart, Staatstheater, 26 February 1977

Le Grand Macabre, opera in two acts (1974–7), 120 min.
libretto by Michael Meschke and the composer after Michel de Ghelderode's play *La balade du Grand Macabre*
eleven principal soloists (*Chef der Geheimen Politischen Politzei* coloratura soprano, *Venus* high soprano, *Amanda* soprano, *Amando* mezzo-soprano, *Fürst Go-Go* boy soprano or high counter-tenor, *Mescalina* dramatic mezzo-soprano, *Piet vom Fass* high buffo tenor, *Nekrotzar* character baritone, *Astradamors* bass, *Weisser Minister* and *Schwarzer Minister* speakers), boys' chorus, two mixed choruses; 3.3.3.2 a sax.3 – 4.5.3.1 – cel (hpd), elec org (regal), pf (elec pf), harp, mandolin, timp, 3 perc – 3.0.2.6.4
* Swedish Royal Opera (Britt-Marie Aruhn *Säpopo*, Monika Lavén *Venus*, Elisabeth Söderström *Clitoria*, Kerstin Meyer *Spermando*, Gunilla Slättergård *Furst Gogo*, Barbro Ericson *Mescalina*, Sven-Erik Vikström *Piet von Sup*, Erik Sæden *Nekrotzar*, Arne Tyrén *Astradamors*)/Elgar Howarth, production by Michael Meschke, designs by Aliute Meczies, Stockholm, 12 April 1978
o Wergo 6170 (Eirian Davies *Chef der Gepopo* and *Venus*, Olive Fredricks *Amanda*, Penelope Walmsley-Clark *Amando*, Kevin Smith *Fürst Go-Go*, Christa Puhlmann-Richter *Mescalina*, Peter Haage *Piet vom Fass*, Dieter Weller *Nekrotzar*, Ude Krekow *Astradamors*, Austrian Radio Choir and Arnold Schönberg Choir, Austrian Radio Symphony Orchestra/Elgar Howarth, 1987)

Le Grand Macabre, revised version (1996), 120 min.
disposition as before except that *Weisser Minister* is a buffo tenor, *Schwarzer Minister* a buffo baritone, and there is no boys' chorus
* Salzburg Festival (Sybille Ehlert *Gepopo* and *Venus*, Ana Maria Martinez *Amanda*, Charlotte Hellekant *Amando*, Derek Lee Ragin *Fürst Go-Go*, Jard van Nes *Mescalina*, Graham Clark *Piet vom Fass*, Ferruccio Furlanetto *Nekrotzar*, Steven Page *Astradamors*, Steven Cole *Weisser Minister*, Richard Suart *Schwarzer Minister*, Vienna State Opera Chorus, Philharmonia)/Esa-Pekka Salonen, production by Peter Sellars, Salzburg, 28 July 1997
o Sony S2K 62312 (musicians of première, 1997)

Scenes and Interludes from *Le Grand Macabre*, 47 min.
concert version for four soloists, chorus ad lib. and orchestra
* Inga Nielsen, Olive Fredricks, Peter Haage, Dieter Weller, Berlin Radio Symphony Orchestra/Elgar Howarth, Berlin, 1979
• Wergo 60085 (soloists of première, Danish Radio Chorus and Orchestra) Elgar Howarth

Mysteries of the Macabre for trumpet and piano (1988), 7 min.
arranged by Elgar Howarth from three arias in the second act
o Philips 426144 (Håkan Hardenberger, Roland Pöntinen, 1989)

Mysteries of the Macabre for trumpet or coloratura soprano and chamber orchestra (1991), 9 min.
arranged by Elgar Howarth from the above
solo tpt or S, 1.1.1.1 – 1.1.1.0 – perc, pf (cel) – 1.1 (mandolin) 1.1.1
* Håkan Hardenberger, Århus Sinfonietta/Elgar Howarth, Århus, 16 March 1992 (trumpet version); Lisa Saffer, New England Conservatory students/John Heiss, Boston,

New England Conservatory, 11 March 1993 (soprano version)
o   Sony SK 62311 (Sibylle Ehlert, Philharmonia/Esa-Pekka Salonen, 1995)

Hungarian Rock (Chaconne) and *Passacaglia ungherese* for harpsichord (1978), 5 min. and 4³/₄ min.

*   Elisabeth Chojnacka, Cologne, 20 May 1978 (*Hungarian Rock*); Eva Nordwall, Lund, 2 February 1979 (*Passacaglia ungherese*)
•   Caprice 1209 (*Hungarian Rock* only: Eva Nordwall); o Wergo 60100 (both pieces: Elisabeth Chojnacka, 1983/4); o Col Legno 031 815 (both pieces: Erika Haase); o Finlandia 367 (both pieces: Jukka Tiensuu); o Sony SK 62307 (both pieces: Elisabeth Chojnacka, 1995); o Sony SK 62310 (*Hungarian Rock* only: Pierre Charial *barrel organ*, 1995)

Hyllning för Hilding Rosenbergs födelsedag (med besvärjandet av Bartóks anda) for violin and cello (1982), 1 min.
o   Sony SK 62306 (Irvine Arditti, Rohan de Saram, 1994)
Trio for violin, horn and piano (1982), 21¹/₂ min.
I. Andantino con tenerezza – II. Vivacissimo molto ritmico – III. Alla marcia – IV. Lamento: Adagio

*   Saschko Gawriloff, Hermann Baumann, Eckart Besch, Hamburg-Bergedorf, 7 August 1982
o   Wergo 60100 (Saschko Gawriloff, Hermann Baumann, Eckart Besch, 1983/4); o Erato ECD 75555 (Maryvonne Le Dizès-Richard, Jacques Deleplancque, Pierre-Laurent Aimard, 1986); o Bridge 9012 (Rolf Schulte, Purvis, Allan Feinberg); o Montaigne 782 006 (Guy Comentale, André Cazalet, Cyril Huvé, 1992); o Sony SK 62309 (Saschko Gawriloff, Marie-Luise Neunecker, Pierre-Laurent Aimard, 1996)

Drei Phantasien (Hölderlin) for sixteen voices (1983), 11 min.
  I. Hälfte des Lebens – II. Wenn aus der Ferne – III.
  Abendphantasie
  * Swedish Radio Chorus/Eric Ericson, Stockholm, 26
    September 1983
  o EMI CDC 7 54096 (Groupe Vocal de France/Guy Reibel,
    1988); o Sony SK 62305 (London Sinfonietta Voices/
    Terry Edwards, 1994)

Magyar etüdök [Hungarian Studies] (Weöres) for sixteen voices
  (1983), 5½ min.
  I. Spiegelkanon – II. – III. Vásár [Fair]
  * Schola Cantorum Stuttgart/Clytus Gottwald, Stuttgart, 18
    May 1983 (nos.1–2); same musicians, Metz, 17
    November 1983 (complete)
  o EMI CDC 7 54096 (Groupe Vocal de France/Guy Reibel,
    1988); o Col Legno 031 830 (musicians of première); o
    Sony SK 62305 (London Sinfonietta Voices/Terry
    Edwards, 1994)

Die grosse Schildkröten-Fanfare vom Südchinesischen Meer
  [The Big Turtle-Fanfare from the South China Sea] for
  trumpet (1985), ½ min.
  o Sony SK 62318 (Håkan Hardenberger, 1996

Etudes for piano (1985–)
  Premier livre (1985): I. Désordre – II. Cordes à vide – III.
  Touches bloquées – IV. Fanfares – V. Arc-en-ciel – VI.
  Automne à Varsovie
  2¼ min., 3 min., 2 min., 3½ min., 3¼ min., 4¼ min.
  Deuxième livre (1988–94): VII. Galamb borong (1988–9) –
  VIII. Fém (1989) – IX. Vertige (1990) – X. Der
  Zauberlehrling (1994) – XI. En suspens (1994) – XII.
  Entrelacs (1993) – XIII. L'escalier du diable (1993) – XIV.
  Coloana infinită (1993) 2¼ min. 2¾ min. 2¾ min. 3min. 3
  min. 3½ min. 1 min.

Troisième livre (1995–): XV. White on White (1995)

* Louise Sibourd, Bratislava, 15 April 1986 (I); Volker Banfield, Warsaw, 24 September 1986 (II – III – VI); Volker Banfield, Hamburg, 1 November 1986 (IV – V); Volker Banfield, Berlin, 23 September 1989 (VII – VIII); Volker Banfield, Gütersloh, 5 May 1990 (IX); Volker Banfield, Schwetzingen, 23 May 1993 (XIII); Pierre-Laurent Aimard, Münster, University, 8 November 1993 (XII – XIV); Pierre-Laurent Aimard, Strasbourg, 6 October 1994 (X); Pierre-Laurent Aimard, Paris, 7 November 1994 (XI, in context of I – XIV); Pierre-Laurent Aimard, The Hague, 26 January 1996 (XV)

o Wergo 60134 (I – VI: Volker Banfield); o Academy ACA 8505 (I – VI: Jeffrey Burns); o Erato ECD 75555 (I Pierre-Laurent Aimard, 1988); o Col Legno 031815 (I – VI: Erika Haase); o Factory FACD 256 (I – VI: Rolf Hind); o Sony SK 62308 (I-XV: Pierre-Laurent Aimard, 1995); o BIS 783 (I-XIV: Fredrik Ullén, 1996)

Etude XIVa 'Coloana fără sfârşit' for player piano (1993), 1 min.

* Jürgen Hocker, Donaueschingen, 14 October 1994
o Sony SK 62310 (Jürgen Hocker, 1995)

Piano Concerto (1985–8), 21½ min.

I. Vivace molto ritmico e preciso – II. Lento e deserto – III. Vivace cantabile – IV. Allegro risoluto, molto ritmico – V. Presto luminoso: fluido, costante, sempre molto ritmico
solo pf; 1.1.1 (ocarina). 1 – 1.1.1.0 – 1-2 perc – 8.7.6.5.4 (or 1.1.1.1.1)

* Anthony di Bonaventura, Austrian Radio Symphony Orchestra/Mario di Bonaventura, Graz, 23 October 1986 (first version I – II – III); same musicians, Vienna, 29 February 1988 (definitive version)
o Sony SK 58945 (Ueli Wiget, Ensemble Modern/Peter Eötvös, 1990); o DG 439 808 (Pierre-Laurent Aimard,

Ensemble InterContemporain/Pierre Boulez, 1992); o
Sony SK 62315 (Roland Pöntinen, Philharmonia/Esa-
Pekka Salonen, 1997)

Der Sommer (Hölderlin) for soprano and piano (1989), 2³/₄ min.
 o   Sony SK 62311 (Christiane Oelze, Pierre-Laurent Aimard,
     1995)

Nonsense Madrigals for six male voices (1988–93), 12 min.
  I. Two Dreams and Little Bat (William Brighty Rands, 1988)
  – II. Cuckoo in the Pear-Tree (William Brighty Rands, 1988)
  – III. The Alphabet (1988) – IV. Flying Robert (Heinrich
  Hoffmann, 1988) – V. The Lobster Quadrille (Lewis Carroll,
  1989) – VI. A Long, Sad Tale (Lewis Carroll, 1993)
 *   The King's Singers, Berlin, 25 September 1988 (I–IV);
     The King's Singers, London, 4 November 1989 (I–V);
     The King's Singers, Huddersfield, 27 November 1993
     (complete)
 o   Sony SK 62311 (The King's Singers, 1996)

Violin Concerto (1989–93), 28¹/₂ min.
  I. Praeludium: Vivacissimo luminoso – II. Aria, Hoquetus,
  Choral: Andante con moto – III. Intermezzo: Presto fluido –
  IV. Passacaglia: Lento intenso – V. Appassionato: Agitato
  molto
  solo vn; 2 (1 rec).1 (ocarina).2 (ocarinas).1 (ocarina – 2.1.1.0
  – 2 perc – 5.0.3.2.1
 *   Saschko   Gawriloff,   Cologne   Radio   Symphony
     Orchestra/Gary Bertini, 3 November 1990 (first version:
     movements 0–IV–III, the first subsequently abandoned);
     Saschko Gawriloff, Ensemble Modern/Peter Eötvös,
     Cologne, 8 October 1992 (second version: movements
     I–II–III–IV–V); Saschko Gawriloff, Ensemble Inter-
     Contemporain/Pierre Boulez, Lyon, 9 June 1993
     (definitive version, with movements III–IV revised)
 o   DG 439 808 (Saschko Gawriloff, Ensemble Inter-

Contemporain/Pierre Boulez, 1993); o Sony SK 62315 (Frank Peter Zimmermann, Philharmonia/Esa-Pekka Salonen, 1997)

Sonata for viola solo (1991–4), 22 min.
I. Hora lungă (1994) – II. Loop (1991) – III. Facsar (1992) – IV. Prestissimo con sordino (1994) – V. Lamento (1994) – Vl. Chaconne chromatique (1994)
* Garth Knox, Vienna, Konzerthaus, 18 November 1991 (II); Jürg Dähler, Geneva, 28 March 1993 (III); Tabea Zimmermann, Gütersloh, 23 April 1994 (complete)
o Montaigne 782 027 (II: première); o Sony SK 62309 (Tabea Zimmermann, 1994)

Bibliography

1 Writings by the composer

'Neue Musik in Ungarn', *Melos*, xvi (1949), pp5–8

'Neues aus Budapest: Zwölftonmusik oder "Neue Tonalität",' *Melos*, xvii (1950), pp45–8

Preface to Philharmonia pocket score of Bartók's Fifth Quartet (Vienna, Universal, [1957])

'Pierre Boulez: Entscheidung und Automatik in der Structure Ia', *Die Reihe*, no.4 (1958), pp38–63; English translation: 'Pierre Boulez: Decision and Automatism in Structure Ia', *Die Reihe*, no.4 (1960), pp36–62

'Zur III. Klaviersonate von Boulez', *Die Reihe*, no.5 (1959), pp38–40; English translation: 'Some Remarks on Boulez' 3rd Piano Sonata', *Die Reihe*, no.5 (1961), pp56–8

'Wandlungen der musikalischen Form' [1958], *Die Reihe*, no.7 (1960), pp5-17; English translation: 'Metamorphoses of Musical Form', *Die Reihe*, no.7 (1965), pp5-19

'Über die Harmonik in Weberns erster Kantate', *Darmstädter Beiträge zur Neuen Musik*, no.3 (1960), pp49-64

'Züstande, Ereignisse, Wandlungen: Bemerkungen zu meinem Orchesterstück "Apparitions",' *blätter + bilder*, no.11 (Würzburg and Vienna, Andreas Zettner, 1960), pp50–57; reprinted in *Melos*, xxxiv (1967), pp165–9

'Die Komposition mit Reihen und ihre Konsequenzen bei Anton Webern', *Österreichische Musikzeitschrift*, xvi/6–7 (1961), pp37–42

'Neue Notation: Kommunikationsmittel oder Selbstzweck?', *Darmstädter Beiträge zur Neuen Musik*, no.9 (1965), pp35–50

'Über neue Wege im Kompositionsunterricht', *Three Aspects of New Music* (Stockholm, Nordiska Musikforlaget, 1968), pp9–44

'Viel Pläne, aber wenig Zeit' [letter to Ove Nordwall of 28.12.1964], *Melos*, xxxii (1965), pp251–2
'Weberns Melodik', *Melos*, xxxiii (1966), pp116–18
'Über Form in der Neuen Musik', *Darmstädter Beiträge zur Neuen Musik*, no.10 (1966), pp23–35
'Bemerkungen zu meiner Orgelstück "Volumina"', *Melos*, xxxiii (1966), pp311–13
'Spielanweisungen zur Erstfassung des zweiten Satzes der "Apparitions"', *Musica*, xxii (1968), pp177–9
'Auf dem Weg zu "Lux aeterna"', *Österreichische Musikzeitschrift*, xxiv/2 (1969), pp80–88
'Auswirkungen der elektronischen Musik auf mein kompositorisches Schaffen', *Experimentelle Musik*, ed. Fritz Winckel (Berlin, Akademie der Künste, 1970), pp73–80
'Apropos Musik und Politik', *Darmstädter Beiträge zur Neuen Musik*, no.13 (1973), pp42–6; English translation: 'On Music and Politics', *Perspectives of New Music*, xvi/2 (1978), pp19–24
'Zur Entstehung der Oper "Le Grand Macabre"', *Melos/Neue Zeitschrift für Musik*, xlv/cxxxix (1978), pp91–3
'Musik und Technik', *Rückblick in die Zukunft* (Berlin, Severin und Siedler, 1981), pp297-324
[Cover drawing featuring cats], *Schweizerische Musikzeitung*, cxxii/4 (1982)
'Aspekte der Webernschen Kompositionstechnik' [1963–4], *Musik-Konzepte Sonderband Anton Webern II* (1984), pp51–104
'Etudes pour piano: Premier livre', with Wergo 60134 (1987); reprinted with Erato ECD 75555 (1990)
'Computer und Komposition: Subjektive Betrachtungen', *Tiefenstruktur der Musik: Festschrift Fritz Winckel zum 80. Geburtstag* (Berlin, 1987), pp22–30
'Zu meinem Klavierkonzert', Programme book, Konzerthaus, Vienna (29.2.1988)
'" . . . nur die Phantasie muss gezündet werden"', *MusikTexte*, no.28–9 (1989), pp3–4

'Ma position comme compositeur aujourd'hui', *Contrechamps*, no.12–13 (1990), pp8–10
'Trio for violin, horn and piano', with Erato ECD 75555 (1990)
'Konvention und Abweichung' [on Mozart's 'Dissonance' Quartet], *Österreichische Musikzeit*, xlvi (1991), pp34–9
'Rhapsodische, unausgewogene Gedanken über Musik, besonders über meine eigenen Kompositionen', *Neue Zeitschrift für Musik*, cliv (1993), pp20–29

2 Interviews with the composer

'Wenn man heute ein Streichquartett schreibt' [Josef Häusler], *Neue Zeitschrift für Musik*, cxxxi (1970), pp378-81; English translation in *Ligeti in Conversation* (London, Eulenburg, 1983), pp102–10
'Interview mit György Ligeti' [Josef Häusler], *Melos*, xxxvii (1970), pp496–507; English translation in *Ligeti in Conversation*, pp83–102
'Fragen und Antworten von mir selbst', *Melos*, xxxviii (1971), pp509–16; English translation in *Ligeti in Conversation*, pp124–37
'György Ligeti' in Ursula Stürzbecher: *Werkstattgespräche mit Komponisten* (Cologne, Gerig, 1971), pp32–45
'György Ligeti gibt Auskunft' [Monika Lichtenfeld], *Musica*, xxvi (1972), pp48–50
'Gustav Mahler und die musikalische Utopie' [Clytus Gottwald], *Neue Zeitschrift für Musik*, cxxxv (1974), pp7–11, 288–95
'Ligeti' [Adrian Jack], *Music and Musicians*, xxii/11 (1974)
'Tendenzen der Neuen Musik in den USA' [Clytus Gottwald], *Neue Zeitschrift für Musik*, cxxxvi (1975), pp266–72
Beszélgetések Ligeti Györgyel [Péter Várnai] (Budapest, Zeneműkiadó, 1979); English translation in *Ligeti in Conversation*, pp13–82
'Entretien avec György Ligeti' [Claude Samuel] in Roland Topor: *Le Grand Macabre* (Paris, Hubschmidt & Bouret, 1981),

pp17–31; English translation in *Ligeti in Conversation*, pp111–23

'Musik mit schlecht gebundener Krawatte' [Monika Lichtenfeld], *Neue Zeitschrift für Musik*, cxlii (1981), pp471–3

'Entretien avec György Ligeti' [Denys Bouliane], *Sonances: revue musicale québecoise*, iii/1 (1983), pp9–27

'Gespräch mit György Ligeti' [Monika Lichtenfeld], *Neue Zeitschrift für Musik*, cxlv (1984),pp8–11

'"The Island is Full of Noise"' [Sigrid Wiesmann], *Österreichische Musikzeitschrift*, xxxix (1984), pp510–14

'Entretiens avec György Ligeti' in Pierre Michel: *György Ligeti: Compositeur d'aujourd'hui* (Paris, Minerve, 1985), pp127–82

'Entretien avec Ligeti' [Edna Politi], *Contrechamps*, no.4 (1985), pp123–7

'György Ligeti über Chancen und Möglichkeiten der Computer-Musik' [Werner Krützfeldt] in *Schnittpunkte, Signale, Perspektiven: Festschrift zur Eröffnung des Neubaus der Hochschule für Musik* (Hamburg, 1986), pp60–61

'Entretien avec Ligeti' [Clytus Gottwald], *InHarmoniques*, no.2 (Paris, IRCAM, 1987), pp217–29

'Geronnene Zeit und Narration: György Ligeti in Gespräch' [Denys Bouliane], *Neue Zeitschrift für Musik*, cxlix/5 (1988), pp19–25

'Stilisierte Emotion' [Denys Bouliane], *MusikTexte*, no.28-9 (1989), pp52–62

'György Ligeti' in Richard Dufallo: *Trackings* (New York, Oxford University Press, 1989), pp327–37

'Ja, ich war ein utopischer Sozialist' [Reinhard Oehlschlägel], *MusikTexte*, no.28–9 (1989), pp85–102

'Colloquy: An Interview with György Ligeti in Hamburg' [Stephen Satory], *Canadian University Music Review*, x/1 (1990), pp101–17

'György Ligeti über eigene Werke: Ein Gespräch mit Detlef Gojowy aus dem Jahre 1988', *Hamburger Jahrbuch für Musikwissenschaft*, xi (1991), pp349–63

'Sur la musique de Claude Vivier' [Louise Duchesneau], *Circuit*,
ii/1–2 (1991), pp7–16
'A Conversation with György Ligeti' [Tünde Szitha], *Hungarian
Music Quarterly* iii/l (1992), pp13–17
'"Ich glaube nicht an grosse Ideen, Lehrgebäude, Dogmen . . ."'
[Lerke von Saalfeld], *Neue Zeitschrift für Musik*, cliv (1993),
pp32–6
'Gespräch über Ästhetik' in Ulrich Dibelius: *György Ligeti: Eine
Monographie in Essays* (Mainz, Schott, 1994), pp253–73
'György Ligeti on his Violin Concerto' [Louise Duchesneau],
Ligeti Letter no.2 (Hamburg, [1995]), pp1–7

3 Monographs, collections and catalogues

*Für György Ligeti: Die Referate des Ligeti-Kongresses,
Hamburg 1988* [= *Hamburger Jahrbuch für Musikwissen-
schaft*, *xi*] (Hamburg, 1991)
Burde, Wolfgang, *György Ligeti: Eine Monographie* (Zurich,
Atlantis, 1993)
– ed., *Komponistenportrait György Ligeti* (Berlin, Berliner
Festwochen, 1988)
Dibelius, Ulrich, *György Ligeti: Eine Monographie in Essays*
(Mainz, Schott, 1994)
Ferguson, Stephen, *György Ligetis Drei Stücke für Zwei Klaviere:
Eine Gesamtanalyse* (Tutzing, Hans Schneider, 1994)
Floros, Constantin, *György Ligeti* (Vienna, Lafite, 1996)
Kollertisch, Otto, ed., *György Ligeti: Personalstil – Avant-
gardismus – Popularität* (Vienna and Graz, Universal, 1987)
Michel, Pierre, *György Ligeti: Compositeur d'aujourd'hui* (Paris,
Minerve, 1985)
Nordwall, Ove, *Ligeti-dokument* (Stockholm, 1968)
– *György Ligeti: Eine Monographie* (Mainz, Schott, 1971)
Restagno, Enzo, ed., *Ligeti* (Turin, EDT, 1985)
Richart, Robert W., *György Ligeti: A Bio-Bibliography* (New
York, Greenwood, 1990)

Sabbe, Herman, *György Ligeti* [*Musik-Konzepte*, no.53]
(Munich, text + kritik, 1987)
Salmenhaara, Erkki, *Das musikalische Material und seine
Behandlung in den Werken 'Apparitions', 'Atmosphères', und
'Requiem' von György Ligeti* [*Forschungsbeiträge zur
Musikwissenschaft*, xix] (Regensburg, 1969)

4 Articles on the Composer

Musik und Bildung, vii/10 (1975) [Ligeti number, including
Siegfried Boris, 'Das kalkulierte Labyrinth', pp.481–9; Rudolf
Frisius, 'Tonal oder postseriell?' pp490–501; Hans-Christian
von Dadelsen, 'Hat Distanz Relevanz? Über Kompositions-
technik und ihre musukdidaktischen Folgen – dargestellt an
György Ligetis Orchesterstück "Lontano",' pp502–6; Wilfred
Gruhn, 'Textvertonung und Sprachkomposition bei György
Ligeti', pp511–19; Sigrun Schneider, 'Zwischen Statik und
Dynamik: Zur formalen Analyse von Ligetis "Atmosphères"',
pp506–10; and Manfred Schuler, 'György Ligeti: "Volumina":
Ein Unterrichtsbeispiel für die Sekundarstufe II]'
Neue Zeitschrift für Musik, cliv/1 (1993) [Ligeti number,
including Stephen Ferguson, 'Tradition – Wirkung –
Rezeption: Anmerkungen zu Ligetis Klaviermusik', pp8–15;
Saschko Gawriloff, 'Ein Meisterwerk von Ligeti: Marginalien
zur Enstehung des Violinkonzerts', pp16–18; Wolfgang Burde,
'Im Banne des imaginären Reichs "Kilviria"', pp42–7]
Bernager, Olivier, 'Autour du Concerto de chambre de Ligeti',
Musique en jeu, no.15 (1947), pp99–101
Bernard, Jonathan W., 'Inaudible Structures, Audible Music:
Ligeti's Problem, and his Solution', *Music Analysis*, vi (1987),
pp207–36
– 'Voice Leading as a Spatial Function in the Music of Ligeti',
Music Analysis, xiii (1994), pp227–53
Beuerle, H.-M., 'Nochmals Ligetis "Lux aeterna"', *Musica*, xxv
(1971), pp279

Bouliane, Denys, 'Les *Six Etudes pour piano* de György Ligeti ou l'art subtil de créer en assumant les référents culturelles', *Canadian University Music Review*, ix/2 (1989), pp36–83; reprinted in *Contrechamps*, no.12–13 (1990), pp98–132

Cadieu, Martine, 'D'un espace imaginaire' [on *Le Grande Macabre* in Paris], *Musique en jeu*, no.32 (1978), pp123–5

Dadelsen, Hans-Christian von, 'Über die musikalischen Konturen der Entfernung: Entfernung als räumliche, historische und ästhetische Perpective in Ligetis Orchesterstück *Lontano*', *Melos/Neue Zeitschrift für Musik*, xliii/cxxxvii (1976), pp187–90

Fabian, I., 'Jenseits von Tonalität und Atonalität', *Österreichische Musikzeitschrift*, xxvii (1973), pp233

Febel, Reinhard, 'György Ligeti: Monument – Selbstportrait – Bewegung (3 Stücke für 2 Klaviere)', *Zeitschrift für Musiktheorie*, ix/l (1978), pp35–51; ix/2 (1978), pp4–13

Gottwald, Clytus, 'Lux aeterna: zur Kompositionstechnik György Ligeti', *Musica*, xxv (1971), pp12–17

Hicks, Michael, 'Interval and Form in Ligeti's *Continuum* and *Coulée*', *Perspectives of New Music*, xxxi/1 (1993), pp172–90

Hoopen, Christiane ten, 'Statische Musik: Zu Ligetis Befreiung der Musik von Taktschlag durch präzise Notation', *MusikTexte*, no.28–9 (1989), pp68–72

Hupfer, Konrad, 'Gemeinsame Kompositionsaspekte bei Stockhausen, Pousseur und Ligeti', *Melos*, xxxvii (1970), pp236–7

Karkoscha, Erhard, 'Eine Hörpartitur Elektronischer Musik', *Melos*, xxxviii (1971)

Kaufmann, Harald, 'Strukturen in Strukturlosen: Über György Ligetis *Atmosphères*', *Melos*, xxxi (1964), pp391–8

– 'Eine moderne Totenmesse: Ligetis *Requiem*', *Neues Forum*, no.13 (1966), pp59–61

– 'Ein Fall absurder Musik: Ligetis *Aventures* und *Nouvelles aventures*', *Spurlinien* (Vienna, Elisabeth Lafite, 1969), pp130–58; French translation in *Musique en jeu*, no.15

(1974) pp75–98; *Spurlinien* also includes the 1964 essay on
Atmosphères, pp107–17
– 'Ligetis Zweites Striuchquartett', *Melos*, xxxvii (1970),
pp181–6
Keller, Hans, 'The Contemporary Problem', *Tempo*, no.89
(1969), pp25–7
Klüppelholz, Werner, 'Aufhebung der Sprache: Zu György
Ligetis *Aventures*', *Melos/Neue Zeitschrift für Musik*,
xliii/cxxxvii (1976), pp11–15
Kropfinger, Klaus, 'Ligeti und die Tradition', *Zwischen Tradition
und Fortschritt*, ed. Rudolf Stephan [= *Veröffentlichungen des
Instituts für neue Musik und Musikerziehung Darmstadt*, xiii]
(Mainz, 1973), pp131–42
Miereanu, Costin, 'Une musique électronique et sa "partition"',
Musique en jeu, no.15 (1974), pp102–9
Morrison, Charles D., 'Stepwise Continuity as a Structural
Determinant in György Ligeti's *Ten Pieces for Wind Quintet*',
Perspectives of New Music, xxiv/1 (1985), pp158–82
Nordwall, Ove, 'Der Komponist György Ligeti', *Musica*, xxii
(1968), pp173–7
– 'György Ligeti', *Tempo*, no.88 (1969), pp22–5
– 'György Ligeti 1980', *Österreichische Musikzeitschrift*, xxxv
(1980), pp67–75
Op de Oul, Paul, 'Sprachkomposition bei Ligeti: 'Lux aeterna',:
Nebst einigen Randbemerkungen zu den Begriffen Sprach und
Lautkomposition', *Über Musik und Sprache*, ed. Rudolf
Stephan [= *Veröffentlichungen des Instituts für neue Musik
und Musikerziehung Darmstadt*, xiv] (Mainz, 1974), pp59–69
Piencikowski, Robert, 'Le Concert de Chambre de Ligeti',
InHarmoniques, no.2 (1978), pp211–6
Piper Clendinning, Jane, 'The Pattern-Meccanico Compositions
of György Ligeti', *Perspectives of New Music*, xxx/1 (1993),
pp192–234
Reiprich, Boris, 'Transformation of Coloration and Density in
György Ligeti's *Lontano*', *Perspectives of New Music*, xvi/2
(1978), pp167–80

Rollin, Robert L., 'Ligeti's "Lontano": Traditional Canonic Technique in a New Guise', *Music Review* (1980), 289–96

Schultz, Wolfgang-Andreas, 'Zwei Studien über das Cello-Konzert von Ligeti', *Zeitschrift für Musiktheorie*, vi (1975), pp97–104

Searby, Michael, 'Ligeti's Chamber Concerto: Summation or Turning Point?' *Tempo*, no.168 (1989), pp30–34

Steinitz, Richard, 'Music, Maths and Chaos', *Musical Times*, cxxxvii/3 (1996), pp14–20; 'The Dynamics of Disorder', *Musical Times* ibid. 5 (1996), pp7–14; 'Weeping and Wailing', ibid. 8 (1996), pp17–22

Stephan, Rudolf, 'György Ligeti: Konzert für Violoncello und Orchester: Anmerkungen zur Cluster-Komposition', *Die Musik der sechziger Jahre*, ed. Rudolf Stephan [= *Veröffentlichungen des Instituts für neue Musik und Musikerziehung Darmstadt*, xii] (Mainz, 1972), pp117–27

Toop, Richard, 'L'illusion de la surface', *Contrechamps*, no.12–13 (1990) pp61–93

Wilson, Peter Niklas, 'Interkulturelle Fantasien: György Ligetis Klavieretüden Nr.7 und 8', *Melos*, lix (1992), pp63–84

Index of Works

173

General Index

African music 106, 117, 127
Altdorfer, Albrecht 94, 111
Arany, János 12
Auer, Leopold 6

Bach, Johann Sebastian 35, 130
  motets 40
  Prelude in C minor 61
  violin sonatas 128
Bartók, Bela 4, 8, 9, 10, 12, 13,
  14, 18, 22, 25, 31, 47, 71, 109,
  130
  Miraculous Mandarin, The 10
  Music for Strings, Percussion
    and Celesta 10
  string quartets 10, 13, 54
Beatles, The 93
Beckett, Samuel 44
Beethoven, Ludwig van 105
  'Eroica' Symphony 97
  Leonore Overture no.3 56
  string quartets 65
Berg, Alban 89, 90
  Lyric Suite 12, 65
Berio, Luciano 21, 38
  Sinfonia 65
Berlioz, Hector 48
Besch, Eckart 104
Bosch, Hieronymus 52, 94
Botticelli, Sandro 94
Boulez, Pierre 13, 21, 30, 38, 99,
  110
  Le marteau sans maître 21, 23
  Piano Sonata no.3 21, 32
  Structures 16, 23–4, 90

Bouliane, Denys 117
Brahms, Johannes 104, 105
Brancusi, Constantin 126
Brazilian music 97, 103–4
Breughel, Pieter 52, 94
Brezhnev, Leonid 87
Britten, Benjamin 10, 11
Bruckner, Anton 59, 83

Cage, John 27, 39, 99
Calonne, Jacques 93
Caribbean music 104, 105, 106,
  127
Carroll, Lewis 68, 70, 113, 114,
  130
Cerha, Friedrich 75
Chopin, Fryderyk 61, 91–2, 121

Debussy, Claude
  'Clair de lune' 124
  Etudes 121, 123
  Feux d'artifice 61, 121
  Isle joyeuse, L' 125
Dibelius, Ulrich 123, 130
Dürer, Albrecht 80

Eichendorff, Joseph, Freiherr von
  104
Eimert, Herbert 16, 22, 23
Escher, M.C. 91
Evangelisti, Franco 23

Farkas, Ferenc 3

Gawriloff, Saschko 127, 129

175

Reich, Steve 91-2
 Piano Phase 61
Riley, Terry 91-2
 Keyboard Studies 61
Robinson, William Heath 78
Romanian music 106, 109, 130
Rossini, Gioacchino 99
Rothko, Mark 36

Schlee, Alfred 38
Schoenberg, Arnold 4, 12, 13
 Five Pieces op.16 57
 Pierrot lunaire 13
 string quartets 12, 13, 14
Schumann, Robert 97, 104, 121, 122
Schweinitz, Wolfgang von 102
Scottish music 97
Seiber, Mátyás 54
Siedentopf, Henning 91
Sierra, Roberto 104
Skelton, Geoffrey 114
South East Asian music 104, 123, 127
Spanish music 97
Stalin, Josef 10
Steinitz, Richard 121
Stockhausen, Karlheinz 13, 16, 21, 22, 23, 30, 38
 Carré 28
 Gesang der Jünglinge 13, 17, 21–2, 23, 26
 Gruppen 22
 Kontra-Punkte 23
 Mantra 90
 Momente 40

Zeitmasze 22
Strauss, Johann II 62
Strauss, Richard 62
Stravinsky, Igor 9, 11, 21
 Octet 71
 Petrushka 8
 Rake's Progess, The 99
 Rite of Spring, The 8, 65
Szymanowski, Karol 128

Topor, Roland 115
Tudor, David 39

Verdi, Giuseppe
 Falstaff 99
 Requiem 48
Veress, Sándor 3
Vivier, Claude 115, 133

Webern, Anton 4, 22, 32, 52
 string quartets 14, 65
Welin, Karl-Erik 36, 91
Wieniawski, Henryk 128
Weöres, Sándor 14, 39–40, 70, 72, 110, 111, 116

Xenakis, Iannis 22, 34, 35, 117
 Metastaseis 28

Ysaÿe, Eugène 128

Zacher, Gerd 59
Zhdanov, Andrey 10